CLOSE TO HOME

Praise for Allisa Bahney

Wasteland

"*Wasteland* is the gritty kind of dystopian novel, with the tenacious, imperfect, and badass kind of heroines that melt me faster than a Popsicle at noon in Death Valley. Floods, fires, climate change, pandemics, and nuclear bombs...Grab a glass of water before you start reading this dystopian gem because if the description of the barren wastelands doesn't make you want to chug it down, you might need it to splash it on your face to calm yourself. The world building is eerily vivid, the characters are complex and compelling, and there is oodles of action. If tales of redemption and enemies to lovers in dangerous times is your jam, well, this series is just what you are looking for."—*Lesbian Review*

Outland

"Breaking out of the gates at a hell for leather pace, *Outland* is an action packed, full throttle sequel to the authors' debut novel, *Wasteland*...As *Outland* draws to a dramatic close, the authors leave no doubt that this is just the beginning of the ultimate war between the Resistance and the NAF, and with emotions already running high, book three is sure to begin with a bang!"—*Queer Lit Loft*

By the Author

Wasteland

Outland

Homeland

Close to Home

CLOSE TO HOME

by

Allisa Bahney

2024

CLOSE TO HOME

ISBN 13: 978-1-63679-661-1

This Trade Paperback Original Is Published By
Bold Strokes Books, Inc.
P.O. Box 249
Valley Falls, NY 12185

First Edition: December 2024

CREDITS
Editor: Barbara Ann Wright
Production Design: Stacia Seaman
Cover Design by Tammy Seidick

Acknowledgments

The biggest thank you to my wife, Courtney, for always allowing me time to create, write, and edit for hours on end. It's a huge undertaking with two little kids at home, but I appreciate it endlessly. Theo, Renn, and I love you forever and a day.

To my parents—a long time ago you two decided to embark on an adventure called parenthood with a large number of children. It's something I never truly understood nor fully appreciated until I became a parent myself. I'm not sure how you did it, but you must have done something right because we are all pretty great adults. Thank you for your support in everything we do.

To my siblings, in-laws, extended family, friends, AA, and current/former colleagues (who are also friends)—this past year has been one of the hardest and most heartbreaking I've ever had to face, but I knew I had a constant support system with all of you while I navigated a way to heal. I will never be able to thank you enough.

To Kristin, Annie, Alex, and Breanna—thank you for reading my messy work and giving me honest and helpful feedback.

Thank you to Bold Stokes Books for continuing to trust me with a keyboard and an idea. A special thanks to Sandy and Ruth for always answering questions. Thanks to my cover artist, Tammy Seidick, for making it beautiful. And a huge thank you to my editor, Barbara Ann Wright, for your patience, critiques, encouragements, and willingness to put necessary words back into the manuscript when I go on a deleting spree.

For Grandpa Butch—fulfilling a promise
I made to him a long time ago.

CHAPTER ONE: GOING HOME

There's supposed to be something magical or romantic about going home again. Especially at Christmas. It's a permanent painting in the back of my mind with snow falling, lights dancing from house to house in various sizes and colors. The decorated trees in the yards, in the windows, and in every community space are a comfort that buries itself deep in the heart. The lyrical way writers and musicians describe this time of year gives it an aura that transcends our basic lives and gives us a few shining moments each year to be better people. People who sing, people who give, people who love.

Then there are the ones who just happen to be going home to the same old shit they've always known home to be. The ones going through the yearly motions with a cloud of humbug hanging above them.

That's me. I'm the same old shit.

I'm a little earlier this year than usual, which will make it damn near impossible to avoid every soul in town. Typically, I'd be driving quietly into my small Iowa hometown just past midnight on the twenty-fourth without a single person aware of my arrival, then back on the road for Minneapolis the evening of the twenty-fifth before my brother could even breathe a word of my presence to anyone in Maple Park.

This year, it's different. I'm heading home early because Grandma died.

Less than a month before Christmas.

I pop my neck to the side to try to release some pent-up tension, knowing I will be forced to not only see everybody I have been so adamantly avoiding for almost twenty years but also interact with them. It's not that I hate anyone from Maple Park, it's just a small town, so they're curious. Or nosy. I was lucky enough to have made a name for myself outside of the sleepy town when I published some books and made some money. Of course, this wasn't until I left in a dramatic fashion the summer after I graduated high school.

The mantra of "everybody knows" is common in a town this size. Everybody knows I lost both my parents. Everybody knows I had my heart broken. Everybody knows I quit my college basketball team. Everybody knows I am a published author. The avoidance has really been me trying to dodge questions. I don't want to talk about my parents or the girl who dumped me, and I certainly don't want to discuss my lackluster basketball career. As my visits became shorter and further apart through the years, I fell away from talking to anyone except for my grandmother during our weekly phone call. The longer I evaded coming home, the more awkward it became for me. Something I am dwelling on alone, as my grandma said a few times. She always claimed it was something I was building up in my mind.

Now everybody knows my grandmother has died. And by extension, everybody knows I'm coming home for her funeral.

My brother, a man over forty still living in Grandma's basement, insisted he needed me to come home as soon as possible, just in case something unforeseen popped up. I honestly think he's scared to be in the house alone. Tommy and I haven't been close for years, but somewhere in my heart, I found a little sympathy for him and agreed to come as quickly as I could. "Quickly" turned out to be four days later. For some reason, I couldn't get myself to commit to coming home any earlier. I know it would have disappointed Grandma, and it sits like a weight in my already heavy heart.

When Mom lost custody of Tommy and me, Grandma didn't even flirt with the idea of us going anywhere else. It couldn't have been easy to take in two kids at her age, but she did it with grace. Our lives were turned upside down in a home with boundaries, rules, and expectations. I'm not thrilled that my mother is a former addict and alcoholic, but her final straw with the law was the best thing that ever happened to my brother and me. Grandma was more than a grandmother. She was everything, including the reason I had enough courage to follow my passion, even if it meant leaving her and Tommy behind after my heart was broken. Her unwavering support kept me pushing forward with my writing until something clicked.

My grip tightens on the steering wheel. The fact that she's actually gone doesn't seem real. I've never come home and not been greeted by a portly woman with white hair. For the first time since hearing the news, I'm actually craving the feeling of being engulfed by her large arms and overwhelmed with the smell of the lilac lotion she loved so much.

I suck in a deep breath through my nose and release it slowly, allowing my eyes to drift shut for just a moment. I try to remember the smell. To recreate it. I feel the vehicle drift slightly and open my eyes.

The autopsy said her heart gave out while she slept. They told Tommy she probably didn't feel it. "Died peacefully in her sleep" is what the obituary reads. I've never given any thought to it, but is dying peacefully even possible? Isn't there some awareness and panic?

My thoughts are interrupted as the town welcome sign comes into view. A smattering of Christmas lights illuminates the dark sky, and a sense of ease washes over me at the sight. Going home feels safe, even when I don't want it to.

As I pull past the city park full of maple trees, I do a quick check of the clock on the dashboard. Winter makes for early nights, but it's barely past eight o'clock as I turn down Main Street and take the familiar path to my childhood home where Tommy is waiting. There are already signs on nearly every light pole and street sign advertising this year's Santa Day festivities. A pang shoots through my chest. Grandma loved Santa Day. It was her favorite part of the Christmas season.

I park in front of the house, not even attempting to hide my vehicle because there's no point. I allow myself another moment to process all this and lay my head on the steering wheel after turning the car off. The heat in the car dissipates almost immediately, and I start to shiver. A coat would have been a great choice. Of all the things to forget in Minneapolis, I forgot my winter coat in the first week of December. I rub my arms and sigh before practically throwing the door open. I grab the duffel from the back seat and sprint up the front steps to the door with my bag slung over my shoulder.

I'm barely over the threshold when a booming voice makes me jump out of my skin. "Why were you sitting in the car?" Tommy asks before the front door is even closed.

"Jesus, Tommy." I jump and grab my chest, briefly wondering if my body actually hit the ceiling as fast as my stomach dropped to my ass. "Why were you standing there watching me?" I pant and attempt to regain my equilibrium.

"I was waiting for you. I have to tell you something." He runs his hands nervously through his shaggy blond hair and scratches at the stubble on his cheeks, which I notice has a tint of gray in it now. I'm not sure when we got so old. It feels like it was just a few years ago I packed my car and left town for good, but now I'm pushing thirty-nine, and Tommy is forty-one. I suppose it makes sense Grandma died, considering our ages. If only math could explain to my heart why it hurts so bad.

Tommy continues to dance from one foot to the other.

"Tommy. Stop. What is it?"

He halts, and his blue eyes finally meet mine. Sometimes, it feels like looking in a mirror. We look so much alike that it's unnerving. I've always worn my hair to at least shoulder length, just so we wouldn't get mistaken as the same person. Tommy's stubble helps. Grandma told me during one of our phone calls it was something he started after turning forty. He's embracing his age, she said.

"Look," he starts, "I know we have a lot to do this week, and there's going to be a lot of running around, but don't be surprised if you see a couple women here."

"I couldn't care less about your girlfriends." I stomp some

snow off my boots and kick them to the side rug. "Are there extra coats in the closet? I forgot mine."

"It's not like that with the women. Not anymore," he continues as I push past him and head toward the stairs and to my old bedroom. "And I'm sure something in the closet will work."

The house feels empty without Grandma's presence, and Tommy is already immensely more annoying without her as a buffer. I catch a glimpse of the decorated tree in the living room. Grandma probably had it up the day after Thanksgiving. The rest of the house is decorated, too. Garland, glass figurines, and endless pictures of Santa Claus replacing the landscapes that adorn the walls the rest of the year. I don't have to see them to know that two interpretive drawings of the North Pole are hung on the refrigerator with Grinch magnets, courtesy of Tommy and me in 1996.

"Eli, wait, I need to explain." Tommy follows me up the stairs, taking two at a time to catch up.

I throw my bag to the side of the room and flop on my old bed. The clean sheets are folded and placed neatly at the end. My throat tightens. Grandma had washed and folded the sheets for me this far before Christmas? I sit back up. "How did it happen? With Grandma?"

He stops in the doorway, his mouth agape like he was about to say something else before my question. "What do you mean?"

"Like, did you find her?" It burns as I swallow and try to keep the tears at bay.

He hesitates. "Well, yeah." He takes a deep breath and lets the air out slowly. I can tell he's hurting. We used to be inseparable. We only had each other to rely on after Dad died and Mom spiraled. Nobody understood what we went through except us. When we drifted apart, it hurt Grandma. She wanted us to stay close so we always had someone to fall back on.

But we grew in separate directions. I left for college, and he stayed. I got a publisher in the city, and he got a job doing lawn care. I closed myself off from the people in my past, and Tommy had a lot of sex. Both very unsafe behaviors, but at least neither of us used our addictive personalities for alcohol or pills. Our shared childhood trauma could have easily spun us in that direction, but Grandma managed to keep us on a somewhat straight path.

"Where?" I ask.

"In her bed." He frowns.

"How did she look?"

"Jesus, Eli, why are you being so morbid?" He steps farther into my room and sits at the empty desk in the corner.

"Did she look at peace? Like maybe she was okay with it?" The thought of her in pain or having any kind of emotions tied to her death is making the guilt of not being here so much worse.

"I don't know. I guess?" He scratches at his chin again. "She looked dead, E. What do you want me to say?"

I want him to tell me she felt no pain and left this world knowing she'd had a good life. I want her to have felt at peace. There was a time when Tommy would have known what I needed to hear. Not anymore. I wonder if this is the last Christmas we'll spend together now that our link is gone. "Nothing. Never mind." I dismiss it with a wave. "What were you saying?"

He sits a little straighter and puffs his chest. "I'm going to be a dad."

I would have been less shocked to hear he's growing a second head. My mouth falls open, and nothing comes out with the first try. In my mind, I'm reeling. I always figured we were too messed up by our own parents to ever be ones ourselves. And as our ages climbed, it just seemed less and less likely. *Okay.* I draw out the word. "Explain."

"Remember Angela Lee?" he asks, a smile on his face.

"Not even a little."

"Oh, come on. You were in the play together your senior year. She had powder in her hair so she could play your mother." He bounces in his seat.

I blink a few times, still shocked he's going to be a dad but even more so at how excited he seems. "You got Old Angie pregnant?"

"Yes," he says excitedly. "We were seeing each other kind of casually, and well, I'm going to be a dad." He claps his hands.

"Awesome." I nod along. "And congrats, I can tell you're excited."

"Nervous, mostly. And there's more." He clears his throat. "I cheated on Angie with Tara Matthews before I knew she was pregnant. Remember her? Tara?"

I rub my forehead. There's the lying, cheating, playboy brother I remember. "Yeah." I sigh. "We played ball together, you know that." I'm fully expecting this story to turn into something about how he's going to have no custody and have to pay child support so he needs money or something. "So Angie is pissed at you and—"

"Oh, yes," he quickly interrupts. "They both are."

"Well, of course they are, you dumbass. Having multiple girlfriends has consequences." I can't feign excitement any longer. He's going to be a father, and it's like he never learned how to be an adult first.

"I already got a lecture from Grandma. I don't need one from you." His tone shifts to condescending.

My heart sinks. "Grandma knew?"

His eyes fall to the floor. "Yeah, she knew about both of them."

"Angie and Tara?"

"No, both babies. You didn't let me finish."

I can literally feel my eyes bulge as he quickly explains how he got both women pregnant in the same month last spring. They're both due before Christmas and are both having a boy.

"Tom—" I stop. I can't even formulate words. "What the hell? You couldn't call anytime in the last how many months and tell me I'm going to be an aunt? Twice? Why didn't Grandma tell me?"

"She said it was my thing to tell. And I don't know. We don't really talk. It's not like you'd come home to see the babies or anything. I figured you'd just see them at Christmas."

The reality of how far apart he and I have fallen settles over the room like a weighted blanket, and it's suffocating. He taught me to ride a bike. He supported me more than our own mother in literally everything. He never missed a single one of my plays, basketball games, or concerts. I went to every single cross-country meet he ran in from seventh grade on. I used to run around within the course like the parents and coaches, cheering him on at every opportunity.

And now he didn't even bother to tell me he's going to be a dad. He's obviously had a hellish year, and I was none the wiser. I swallow hard. "Was Grandma excited? About the babies?"

His eyes well up. "Yeah. Yeah, she was."

"I'm sorry I didn't know." The confession falls past my lips before I can stop it.

It takes him by surprise, too, if his frown is any indication. "How could you? I didn't tell you."

I sigh. "I'm going to unpack. I'll come down so we can discuss tomorrow in a bit."

He nods solemnly and leaves without a response.

I stay on the bed and look around. Grandma left everything the way it was when I was in high school. Old pictures of friends line the mirror over my dresser, and my basketball jersey and shoes sit in a shadow box collecting dust in a corner. Even the Neve Campbell poster I hung up in sixth grade remains attached to the wall above my nightstand. My eyes land on the framed picture that has been lying facedown next to my lamp for almost twenty years. I know Grandma cleaned my room weekly. She would dust under the picture and then place it back where I'd left it. In all the times I've visited, I've never bothered to lift it or move it.

Avoiding the picture, I observe the rose-colored walls I once loved. I picked out the color myself, and at the time, it felt like the coolest thing Grandma ever let me do. But now, it doesn't really match my personality anymore. Things change, people grow, and my bedroom could use some new paint.

Maybe even a new picture on the nightstand.

I wiggle my fingers above the back of the frame, daring myself to glance under it and look back in time at the faces of two girls about to fall in love at seventeen.

I roll my fingers into a fist and pull my arm close to my chest.

Not yet.

Christmas Eve, seven years ago

"Eli, will you come in here and help me, please?" Grandma's voice echoes through the house.

I'm in the kitchen sneaking some of her homemade chocolate peanut butter balls meant for the children's concert at church later in the evening. "Yeah," I call back around a cheek full of the snack. I make my way into the living room and find her on the floor sitting with her legs pretzel-style. "What in the world are you doing?"

"I saw a present that wasn't wrapped properly, so I got down here to fix it, but now my legs are asleep, and I can't get back up." She laughs at herself.

"You shouldn't be getting down on the floor. I'll fix any presents that need it." I bend and put my arms under hers to lift. Slowly, we get her back to a standing position, but I don't let go until I know she has her balance. "You good?"

"Dr. Reese thinks I'll need a cane soon."

I release her. "Tell Dr. Reese to mind her own business."

She nudges me. "Oh, Eli, stop it. She's never steered me wrong." She slowly lowers herself into her favorite recliner. The thing squeaks like a dying rabbit the moment it has any weight on it. I begged Tommy to fix it last Christmas, but he likes that it makes noise because then he knows when she's trying to get up and move around the house.

I settle on the couch across the room and reach for the remote. "Do you wanna watch a Christmas movie? A funny one?" It's one of my favorite Christmas traditions I haven't given up on yet.

"Yes, but not one with all those cuss words. I know you enjoy throwing those around, but I'm too old for such filth."

"Since when?" I ask, actually perplexed. Grandma can cuss with the best of them.

"Oh hush." She swats at the air between us. "And don't think I didn't smell peanut butter on your breath. Those are for church, young lady."

I curl my lips in between my teeth. Busted. There's a comfortable silence between us as I settle on *Home Alone 2: Lost in New York*. "There. A classic that's funny without bad words."

She squints at the TV. "Ah, yes, I do like this one." She pulls the lever to recline her seat and unfolds the blanket on the arm over her legs. "We have a few hours before I need to get ready. This is nice."

I settle into the couch and pull the quilt from the back, fully prepared to listen to her quote this entire movie. It's one of her favorite things. A movie buff through and through, she loves when we rewatch the same movies over and over. "Where's Tommy? I haven't seen him since I got here."

"He's at his girlfriend's until later tonight."

"Ah. A new one. How long have they been an item?"

"Oh, you know, not long. And won't be much longer, probably."

I snort a laugh. "I'm leaving tomorrow night, so it's his ass if I don't see him."

She's quiet for a moment, and then I hear an exaggerated sigh. It's the one she does when she wants to say something. "Eli?"

"Yeah?"

"Why do you only come home for such a short amount of time?"

"I'm just really busy," I say on autopilot. It's always my go-to excuse.

"You can't fool me. People make time for their families around the holidays. You can't tell me it's any different in Minnesota than Iowa."

Busted again. "Truly, Grandma, I wish I could stay longer," I lie.

"Well, can you come another month? I don't mind the calls, but it's just not the same, honey. I want you here. I sleep better when you're both under my roof. I'm not asking you to move home, just to consider giving us more time. You don't even come to Santa Day anymore."

"You can always come visit me, Grandma," I suggest with a bit of indignation.

"It's pretty difficult for me to make a trip like that." She motions to her legs.

Immediately, I feel bad for the way I spoke to her. "I understand. I'll find some time to come visit." I know I'll be leaving tomorrow evening and not return until next Christmas Eve, just like I have for the past few years. I'll give the same excuses, play the same lie, and do the same thing again and again and again. It hurts me to lie to her but not as much as it hurts to be in a town with so many memories of the people I've lost.

"Thank you, darling. I love you."

"Love you, too, Grandma."

We settle in and watch as Kevin gets on the wrong airplane. Only a few moments have passed when Grandma claps her hands with excitement, "Oh! I forgot to tell you I finished your book. I feel so privileged getting to read the sequel before it's officially published."

"And? What did you think?"

"Is that missing boy dead or alive?"

"Grandma. Spoilers. I'm not going to give that away."

"Oh fine." She swats at the air again. "How many more books are going to be in the series?"

"I'm not sure yet. And what did you think? The anticipation is—"

"I loved it, sweetie. Of course I did." She smiles at me and looks back to the television. "I see lots of you in some of those scenes," she continues without looking at me.

"What do you mean?"

"Well, good writers write what they know, right?"

"Yeah, I suppose."

"You're writing what you know, and since I'm your grandma, I can tell."

I frown at her. "Grandma, the book is set in the 90s and has witches and time travel and curses and hauntings. It's all fantasy."

"Obviously, dear," she says with a sarcastic tone. "I mean the human parts. The love story, the family, and the town. All very familiar, don't you think?" She winks.

"It's fiction, Grandma. This all came from the deep recesses of my brain. It has literally nothing to do with Maple Park."

"Okay, honey, if you say so." She turns her attention back to the television. "Or maybe you miss your hometown and subconsciously project it through your writing?"

I pinch the bridge of my nose. "Sure, whatever you say."

Excerpt from The Stone River Series by Eli Thomas

Book One: The Curse

Not much could shake up Joey. Working as a school counselor for well over a decade had pretty much numbed all her inhibitions. But whenever Sidney, the mouthy school resource officer, invaded her space, Joey found herself unsteady. She had spent the better part of the last two years trying to convince herself that she was simply annoyed by the woman in uniform, and it had nothing at all to do with the fact that she was so desperately intrigued by her.

Joey would typically be enjoying her time alone in the teachers' lounge this far past the last bell, but with the recent vandalism, the missing teenager, and now the power surges, it's not a surprise Sidney is patrolling the school this late in the day. Joey concludes she is probably hoping to overhear students talking about Mason or that he'll magically appear and come back to a familiar place... like school.

She shifts uncomfortably in her seat as Sidney strides past her to the refrigerator. Sidney clears her throat as she opens the door and looks inside. "You're here kind of late, Campbell."

Joey mashes her lips together and debates if this is small talk or an interrogation since her niece, Abby, is Mason's best friend, and Joey has been Abby's legal guardian for years. Either way, not answering is making this silence suspicious and awkward. "I stay late most days, actually. I like to get caught up on work while Abby has her music lesson." The awkward silence expands. Joey nervously bounces her knees. "I was looking through Mason's file and the notes I've kept on him to see if anything might help." She lays it all out there, hoping that'll ease any suspicions Sidney may hold against her.

Sidney takes a container out of the refrigerator and walks to the microwave. "And how's that going for you?"

"I'm not finding anything," she answers honestly.

"Yeah, nobody is. But you didn't hear that from me." She turns and smiles. "What are you having for dinner?" She motions to Joey's container.

"Oh." She looks at the cold mush. "It's leftover spaghetti, I think."

Sidney laughs. "You think?" The microwave beeps, and she removes her own food.

The smell of fresh peppers pulls at Joey's senses, and she sits up straighter. "Yours smells so good. What is it?"

Sidney joins her at the table. "Fajita stir fry. Want to try some?"

She does. She very much does, but she's not going to admit that. "Oh, uh, no, thanks. I'm actually full from my possible spaghetti mush."

Sidney takes a dramatically large bite and then unleashes an exaggerated moan. "Now, that's delicious. Too bad you're so full."

Joey bites her bottom lip to keep from laughing. She can feel her cheeks warm while wondering if Sidney is actually flirting with her. It's not out of the realm of possibility but highly unlikely, given she doesn't know many people who are like herself, especially not in a small town like Stone River. She's had to meet all her past girlfriends and lovers at the lone gay bar in the downtown area of the capital city. Even that's a risk because she never knows when she may accidentally see a former student or parent. She's done quite well keeping her sexuality a secret for nearly forty years and manages to dodge the "why aren't you married" questions like a pro. She has high hopes for the future generations and that they'll be more accepting, but in 1996, there's still a reason to hide.

She looks at Sidney for a moment too long and gets caught in the process. "Sorry," she blurts.

"Do I have food on my face?"

"No, I was just spacing out. I'm sorry." She looks at her watch

and stands. "I need to go get Abby from her lesson. It was nice talking to you, Officer Cruz, and I'll let you know if I find anything helpful on Mason."

Sidney nods, but Joey doesn't miss the disappointment etched across her face. Now she wants to backtrack and stay with her a bit longer, but it's too late. "It was nice having someone to talk to for a bit, so thank you, Joey."

Joey's breath catches. Sidney has never used her first name before. They haven't had very many interactions over the years but have always been aware of each other's presence. This is new. Bold. "Uh, yeah," Joey replies with a slight tremor in her voice. "Let's do this again."

"I'd like that." She smiles. "And you can call me Sidney."

Joey trips over her own feet trying to leave before Sidney can see her blush. She was definitely flirting.

CHAPTER TWO: SAYING GOOD-BYE

The visitation for Grandma is simple but busy. My best guess is Tommy and I have shaken hands and accepted awkward hugs from nearly two hundred people, and it's not even half over. At least the swarm of affection has distracted me from the open casket only a few feet from where I'm standing.

The mortician did a wonderful job, truly. Grandma looks like herself for the most part. She's wearing her same shade of lipstick and an old lady blazer she picked out years ago to be her funeral attire. The day she told me it was the outfit she wanted to be buried in, I asked her why old people did such weird things like picking out their own funeral clothes. She shrugged and said there were so few things we can control in life, especially near the end, but that was one we still had a say in. She would be happy to know we followed her wishes.

Before we started this circus, Tommy and I had to agree on her obituary and funeral program. It was pretty simple since she had most of that planned as well. I was glad to see she opted to include the poem she wrote in her obituary. I'm sure most people won't understand, but she did it for me.

After another overly aggressive back pat and a breathy whisper into my ear, I nearly lose my mind over the nauseating and endless repetition of sentiments:

Sorry for your loss.

She was a wonderful woman.

I'm praying for you.

Over and over and over again.

Avoiding the urge to roll my eyes, I keep saying thank you and offering the barest smile to each person. I recognize most of the people, but I can't place a name with everyone. Like every small town, there are a few unforgettable ones. Like Mr. Hanon, a twice-retired school administrator who is always coated with a thin layer of sweat from his bald head to his damp palms. I do a double wipe on my pants after shaking his hand. He had my father as a student and has reminded me of this at every opportunity since I was fourteen. Not far behind him is Sara, the former cheerleader. She was a senior when I was a freshman and is still the loudest person I've ever met. Even when I brace myself for her condolences, I still jump at the sheer volume of her voice. Then there's one of the Taylor twins, whose first name I can't place. He sheepishly hands me a business card for his 3D printing business. Alan the ATV guy. Marlene the giggler. John the farmer. Erin the booster club president. Kait the gossip. BJ the bartender. Wendell the grocer. The list goes on and on.

I'm on edge and anxious, much to my annoyance. It's not because I'm heartless or hate my hometown, I just don't want to see *her*.

Aracely Hernandez.

A flood of emotions fills me to every nerve ending at just the thought of her. Every single person from my past has somehow linked themselves to Aracely in my subconscious, and being home makes me feel like I can't escape an inevitable reunion with the girl who has defined so much of me.

I know she moved away from Maple Park at some point, but I also know she visits around the holidays. If she's in town, she's going to come to this visitation.

She loves my grandma.

Loved.

I stretch my neck side to side as I take another hand and another offered prayer. It's an adjustment to think of Grandma in the past tense. Tomorrow will mark the first week that we haven't spoken since I moved away. I can already feel the absence of her voice echoing in my mind. It feels like I've lost a piece of me I selfishly thought I'd have forever.

Tommy leans toward me. "Aracely is here. She's near the back of the line."

I appreciate the warning and let him know with a quick nod. It's one of those rare occurrences where I'm genuinely grateful for my brother. He really does care about me, and as we are practically the same, I'm not shocked that his next sentence is a plea to let him know if I see either of his baby mamas come through the door.

I glance at the back of the line, and I'm just about to ask when he answers my next question for me. "She lives back home now. Been here for a few years."

I don't really process what he's said before my stomach flips, and I barely catch a glimpse of Aracely's dark hair as she steps inside from the cold. Her face and most of her body is blocked by the rest of the people, but it's definitely her. I would know those large, wavy locks anywhere. I'm baffled by how quickly my "I don't want to see her" turns into me craning my neck to catch a glimpse of the face between those waves. I can see the right side of her as she rubs her arms and shakes the cold from her body.

Until this moment, I haven't actually considered how long people are waiting in the winter chill to pay their respects to Grandma. I find the patience in the cold to be more genuine respect than the mundane and repeated phrases. I would walk through a blizzard barefoot for my grandmother, but seeing it from friends and acquaintances is a truly remarkable testament to her.

I reach for the next hand but keep my eyes trained on the back of the line, wondering what in the hell I'm going to say to Aracely when she makes her way up here. It's me who is grieving, so it should be on the other person to speak first. I've been mumbling a chorus of thank-yous for the past two hours, so maybe I'll just say that.

Another hand gets thrust in my direction and pulls my focus back to what's going on in front of me. I vaguely hear Tommy having a conversation with someone whose name I can't remember while I shake their disgustingly moist hand.

After they finally move on, I glance to the back of the line again, only to find Aracely has disappeared. For a brief moment, I consider maybe she thought better of it and stepped out. Maybe this isn't the best place for a reunion after over twenty years. If anybody has the wherewithal to know that, it's Aracely. Although we did see each other a few years after the breakup. I squint and attempt to navigate my brain to the year I saw her at Christmastime. It was the reason I started sneaking into and out of town so quickly. I hated that I was blindsided by seeing her so happy while I was still so miserable. Clearly, the heartbreak hadn't been even, and that moment made it more obvious than ever before.

Another handshake. Another I'm sorry.

I think it was eleven years ago. Maybe twelve. A little more than a "few" years, I suppose.

Another hand. Another empty promise to pray for me.

We saw each other in the grocery store. I had just been published, and I was so bitter that nobody cared I was home I could barely function. I couldn't get away from her fast enough. I didn't want to speak to anybody that day but especially not my ex-girlfriend with her own *new girlfriend* on Christmas Eve. She wanted to talk to me and practically chased me out of the store and into the winter cold, just to get my attention. I didn't give her a chance. I kept walking. I left my car there and walked back to Grandma's after fighting with both Tommy and Grandma in public. My fingers and toes were frostbitten for weeks after. Not my proudest moment.

Handshake. Sorry for your loss.

I scan the funeral home again to no avail. Aracely isn't here anymore. She definitely decided to leave. It's probably better this way, but I can't help the immediate and painful grief that settles in my chest. Grandma isn't here, and now, neither is Aracely.

I accept the next hand without even looking at the person.

"Thank you," I repeat robotically.

"I haven't said anything yet," comes a casual response with a hint of amusement. A voice I'd never mistake.

I focus on the face in front of me. "Aracely, hi," I mumble as I awkwardly pull my hand back.

"Are you looking for someone in particular?" she asks with an eyebrow raised. She motions around the room with a single finger.

"Uh, no. I was just"—I wave my hand—"spacing out a bit. There are a lot of people here." I look at my feet in an attempt to hide my embarrassment. Before I can think of something else to say, I'm nearly knocked over with the force of Aracely grabbing my shoulders with both hands. She does a weird move where I think she's going to hug me, then thinks better of it.

"Eli, I don't even know what to say," she says with sadness laced around every word. "I just saw her at the post office last week. I can't believe it."

Grandma. That's why Aracely is here. Not for me. I don't know why I thought that for even a second. I know better. She made it clear a long time ago we are not on the same path in life. I can tell she's genuinely upset.

"Well, you can borrow one of the things I've heard about a hundred times already. Just tell me you're so sorry, and she was a wonderful person."

She swipes at a few stray tears. "What, no thoughts and prayers?"

"Please don't."

"Thought that one might be your favorite by now." She winks, and I choke on whatever witty response I may have.

"Tommy's favorite," I manage and roll my eyes. It's nice to not have to hide my utter disdain for organized religion for a moment. Aracely never judged me for not believing in any of it. In return, I never judged her *for* believing it.

"*Well.*" She draws out the word. "I better not keep holding up this line. People are outside all the way around the block."

"Seriously?" I ask, half shocked and half disappointed that I'm going to be here so much longer.

She nods. "It was nice seeing you." She turns to make her way to Tommy and then whispers, "How long are—"

"Hi, Aracely," Tommy interrupts.

Her head snaps back to him, and the line moves along, taking her with it. "Hi, Tommy." She leaps forward to hug him. Jealousy consumes me over him getting such an open and affectionate greeting.

I shake my head and turn to the next person in line to accept the elusive prayers everybody keeps throwing around. I wish I could say I'm shocked at how quickly I turned into a puddle of mush over Aracely, but it would be a lie. She's a large part of the reason I avoid this town. I've never quite learned how to behave near her, especially since she decided we were better off apart than together.

What feels like an eternity later, the line is finally dwindling. It's ten minutes before we plan to close the doors and meet with the funeral director, whose name I cannot remember, about tomorrow morning's funeral when I see Pete Kelley walk in.

Pete hasn't changed much since high school, other than the typical aging additives. His waistline is a little bigger, hairline a little farther back, and there are noticeable wrinkles around his eyes. His dark hair is slicked back into a ponytail, and a neatly trimmed goatee adorns his chin. Always proud of his Puerto Rican roots, Pete wears a small pin of the PR flag on every outfit he's ever owned.

He approaches me and pinches his lips together in a sad smile. "Hey, Eli." He goes for a hug that I gladly accept.

"Hey, Pete." I pull back and look him up and down. "You look fancy." I flip a finger under his black tie before flicking the top of the pin.

He makes a show of straightening his shoulders and giving me his best businessman pose. "I'm the high school principal now. I need to look the part at all times."

I award him a long, low whistle and slow clap. "Look at you. Always leveling up."

"As are you. I just finished the first two books in your series for the second time. Quite a feat considering they're both over four hundred pages long." His eyes sparkle with pride. I'm not sure if it's pride that he knows a quasi-famous author or that he's read the fantasy novels.

"Liar."

He feigns shock. "I bought three sets for the school library, and they're featured in a section for local authors. The students love them. They're always checked out."

"I already like you, Pete, don't be a try-hard." Pete is one of the few people back home who I don't mind seeing on the rare occasion I'm in town. He and I were permanent lab partners in science class, and it turned into a true friendship. One of those that transcends time and distance. He will occasionally send me memes, videos, and reels of things he thinks will make me laugh. I do the same for him, and when we actually do happen to see each other, which has been over ten years now, we talk like no time has passed.

"I'm serious. People love mystery and drama." He nudges my shoulder. "So when's the third book coming out?"

"Next fall."

"There's been quite the wait for this one."

It's a harmless comment but a familiar one that digs into my already tender ego when it comes to my release schedule. There are no rules as to how long between installments other than I have to finish the series within fifteen years from the day I signed. After the huge success of the first book, I was adamant I had to get the second book absolutely perfect in order to keep my audience. It took me two years to perfect my rough draft of the first book and four more years to finish my second. It's been thirteen years since I was signed, eleven since I was first published, and seven since the second book was released. For the past two years, I've been fielding calls nearly every week asking about the third book. At one point, I thought I might be able to do a fourth, but now I'm strapped for time and at a severe loss when it comes to writing the ending.

"Yeah," I reply as casually as I can muster. "Publishing dates are weird." I play it off flippantly, banking on his ignorance about how it all works.

He leans in and lowers his voice. "How's it end? Do they find Mason?"

"Pete." I swat at him. "How dare you?"

He holds his hands up in surrender. "All right, all right, fine. I'll wait for it to come out."

"You and everybody else." Including me. My editor and I keep pitching ideas, but nothing sticks.

Grandma comes to mind. She had listened to me complain about finding the right ending for years now. "I wish Grandma had a chance to read the last one." I don't mean to say it out loud, but I'm comfortable with Pete, and it passes my lips before I can stop it.

His smile falls. "I'm really sorry about Elisabeth."

"Yeah." I release a breath so deep and long, it makes my chest ache. "Me too."

To his credit, he handles these types of moments exceptionally well. He gently squeezes my arm in reassurance. "How long are you in town? Wanna grab a beer?"

I laugh despite feeling I may actually start crying, something I have yet to do. "I don't think I'll be around long enough, but thank you."

"Oh, come on. I'll invite some of the old crew, and you can brag about being a best-selling author to people you went to high school with."

"I don't want to brag about anything," I answer honestly.

He fakes a dramatic gasp. "All right, you win. But if you change your mind and stay for a while longer, I might have a proposition for you."

"I'm not sticking around, but I'm insanely curious now." I frown and do a quick check to make sure nobody else has walked in last minute, and we're not holding up a line. Tommy is talking to the funeral director across the room, and most everyone has cleared out.

"A job opportunity. To sub at the high school." His statement brings my attention back to him.

"Never. Pete, you're joking, right?" I can't help the condescending tone or the utter disdain dripping from my words. "I would rather, and I need you to hear this part, drag my head across the carpet until the skin burns off my face than be a substitute teacher at a high school."

"Wow. Graphic." His eyebrows rise with an amused smile. "I think you should add that line into the final book. You have my number if you change your mind." He waves and steps backward to leave.

"I won't." I shake my head. "But thanks for coming."

❖

The next morning, as I'm standing at the back of the only Lutheran church in town, about to follow the casket for the procession up the aisle, the reality of losing my grandma finally lands.

The funeral director, whose name still escapes me, turns to Tommy and me. "Just double-checking that you want only the two of you following the casket. No more next of kin?"

"Our dad was her only child, and Grandpa died when Eli was just a baby. I think there are some nieces and nephews or cousins in there if you'd like them to walk, too," Tommy offers.

"No, no. The two of you are fine, I just didn't want to start if someone was missing." The funeral director holds up his hands to show he's not trying to overstep.

I dry swallow at the mention of Dad and wonder how Grandma managed to live so many years after losing her only child. The thought barely skims the surface of my brain before a memory of her nails combing through a twelve-year-old Tommy's hair resurfaces without warning. Tears spring to my eyes.

"You look so much like him." Her voice breaks, and her eyes shift to me. "You both do."

It's mere seconds before I need to walk in front of practically half the town and sit at the front of the church that I finally feel the urge to cry. I don't understand my hang-up about crying, but it's overwhelming. I have yet to shed a single tear over losing Grandma.

I quickly wave my hands in front of my eyes to dry the moisture and attempt to focus on something else. Anything else. At first, I couldn't cry, and now, I don't want to.

The funeral director breaks into the silence, and I'm grateful. "There are a lot of people. We've had to add folding chairs to the end of each aisle and offer standing room."

It was the exact statement I needed to hear to shift all my emotions from sad to dread. That's so many people looking at me. People who haven't set eyes on me in two decades. I resist the urge to touch my body in places that are different now or to cover the wrinkles near my lips.

It's ridiculous to think anybody in their late thirties would look exactly the same as they did as a teenager, but I can't seem to silence the self-conscious side of me. The guests were funneled in through a side entrance and seated from there, so I can only guess as to who I'll see when they open these doors and usher us in. I'm sure there will be all the hallmarks of a small-town funeral. People from her book club, card club, the church, the school, and so on. Grandma was everywhere. She had contacts and friends in every corner of the community, so it doesn't surprise me it's so full, but it does unnerve me.

I run my palms over my pants and take a few deep breaths in an attempt to calm my pounding heart.

"Oh wow," Tommy says. "Do you think Mom is here?"

"I truly hope not," I say with complete honesty.

"Be nice."

I frown, about to remind him why I'm entitled to my reaction before we're interrupted. "Okay, the pastor is ready." The funeral director guides us to where we'll be following Grandma's casket through the church. "Walk a few paces behind and sit in the front row. It has a Reserved sign on it."

The double doors open, and we begin to amble forward. I can't even see the crowd of faces yet, and I already hear Tommy sniffling. I glance at him, and I'm actually surprised to see tears running deep tracks down his cheeks and dripping from his chin. For a moment, I'm annoyed he's such a sympathetic sight. Poor Tommy, everybody will think. Look at his sister. Not a single tear. Heartless.

"I'm really gonna miss her, Eli," he says without looking at me.

I soften and take his hand. The last time we held hands was at Dad's funeral. I know Tommy remembers it by the soft sob that bubbles out of his throat. He keeps his eyes forward. Somehow, this feels a lot weightier than Dad's funeral. Maybe it's because we were so young and weren't completely comprehending it. Maybe it's because it led to the whirlwind downfall of our mother so we didn't have time to grieve as much. Or maybe it's because way more of my memories revolve around the grandmother who raised me, and I have a lot fewer of my father.

I look at him a second time before we walk in, just to make sure he's steady enough to get through this part. He's wearing a suit and tie. His shaggy blond hair is slicked back, and his stubble has been trimmed. His light blue eyes, normally vibrant, are darker today, and I can actually see his age. For as much as we rarely make time for each other, right now, I feel for him.

We take our first steps into the meeting area of the church and are greeted with a sea of sad faces. Whatever I was expecting a large crowd to be, this is even bigger. I only remember flashes of Dad's funeral, but I definitely don't remember this many people. There were a lot, sure. He was young and died from a brain aneurysm so suddenly.

I'm shaking, and I'm sure Tommy thinks it's from grief, but losing Grandma is the last thing on my mind right now. I do one sweep over the crowd as we march forward. Immediately, I regret it. There are so many familiar people that I can't even begin to place them all. Old classmates, teammates, family friends, neighbors, acquaintances, distant relatives, people from various places in the community, and some I wouldn't recognize if I tried. We saw a lot of people last night, but it was easier to absorb one at a time, not all at once.

I drop my eyes back to what's in front of me and focus on getting Tommy to our seats.

We're almost there when a hand shoots out into the aisle and gently grips my elbow.

Aracely.

"I'm right here," she offers quietly so nobody else can hear it.

I keep my eyes trained in front of me and push forward. I'll relax once we're sitting and Grandma's casket is centered at the front.

The great-aunts and great-uncles who will be seated directly behind us come into view. They all came to the house last night to offer us food, money, and condolences. Most mentioned they are leaving and heading back to their normal lives after today. Grandma was the only one of her siblings to plant roots in Maple Park, so a lot of her family are at least an hour's drive away.

Once I'm seated, I finally relax and release Tommy's hand. He turns to me. "You good?"

"Yeah," I lie. I know how narcissistic it is to believe that some of these people showed up to get a peek at me and not for Grandma. Maybe I've been buried in fictional worlds for so long that I really have turned into a monster. I'm not sure when my anxiety over seeing people from my past started exactly. I know it has to do with feeling like they're going to ask me about what big thing I'm doing next when I honestly don't know. Or ask me about how the series ends, which I also don't know. Or why I quit playing ball when I had it laid out in front of me. Or why I never visited my own grandmother who is now dead. The truth lies somewhere between what others believe the reasons to be and the lies I tell. I waited so long to reconnect with anyone from here, it only serves to remind me of what I've lost. I haven't wanted to come back because I don't fit in this town anymore. It is a very large part of my past that I remember fondly, but it is not my future.

When the opening song ends and I hear the wave of sniffles, soft cries, and blowing noses behind me, I feel like a dick for even considering that anyone here has ulterior motives. Grandma was beloved. Adored. I'm a cynical deserter. The one who ran because her heart and ego simultaneously broke.

Tommy leans toward me and whispers, "Before I forget, Grandma's attorney wants to meet with us at her office about the estate planning this afternoon."

Grandma didn't have much to leave, but I know she's leaving Tommy her house and property and giving me her classic 1962 Starfire Convertible. It needs some work, but it still runs, and I have the money to get it restored. It was Dad's car originally. He always wanted to fix it up and change the paint from robin's-egg blue to a hot red. It's been sitting in Grandma's garage for almost thirty years, and I'm finally taking it with me. I've wanted that car since I was old enough to drive, and Tommy has never even considered moving out of her house. Especially now with two babies on the way, he'll need the space without the mortgage.

Grandma's last gifts to us. Stability for Tommy and a final exit strategy for me. I feel better knowing I'll be on my way out of town with my newly acquired classic car sooner rather than later. If nothing else, I can get through this funeral for that.

❖

"This has to be a mistake." Tommy's voice is hollow. He's in shock. Not only have these past two days been a whirlwind of grief and anxiety, but now we can also throw a sucker punch into the mix.

A punch thrown by our dead grandmother's fist.

"It's not a mistake, Tommy. I had her triple-check everything," Lara says. She's been grandma's attorney since taking custody of us. I trust her wholeheartedly, and that's what makes this even more confusing.

I clear my throat. "When did she write this again? The last will and testament stuff?"

"Well." Lara shuffles some papers. "She updated it a few times over the years as it made sense. When you two became legal adults, there was no need to appoint you another guardian in the event of her death." She shrugs like she isn't sure how much more she can say. She's the executor of the will. She's only doing her job. "The last update was eleven years ago."

"So she messed up. She clearly messed up. A lapse of judgment or something," I say, frustrated.

"I assure you, this is what she wanted." I catch a hint of hesitation, almost like she wants to say more but knows she shouldn't.

"Please say it again," Tommy begs for the fourth time.

Lara sighs and lifts the paper. "I, Elisabeth Thomas, being of sound mind and—"

"Skip to the part," I request, annoyed.

Lara sighs, probably fed up with us. "She left you the house, Eli." She drops the papers. "And you get the car, Tommy. The remaining money and investments she had will be split fifty-fifty. I'm sorry, but that's just how it is."

"I'm sorry, Lara," Tommy says softly. "This is just really confusing for us. Do you know why she did this? I've lived in that house for almost my entire life. I just—"

"I can't discuss that with you, Tommy. She requested it be done and nothing else be shared." We're both silent. Unmoving. "Now, if you two will excuse me, we can get papers signed and things squared away later this week." She stands and exits quickly. Probably to get away from us. The two petulant adults who want to know why their dead grandma chose to play around with their emotions when she's not here to answer any questions.

Tommy swivels in his chair. "Why would she do this, E?"

I drop my head into my arms on the round conference table. I'm sure the entire office is just waiting for us to leave. "I don't know." I lift my head and rub my eyes. "I don't know. There has to be a reason."

"Seriously?" His annoyance is palpable. "It's a mistake. Obviously, we'll just switch. I'll stay here in the house, and you can have the stupid car. It's just taking up space in the garage, anyway."

"Tommy. When have you ever known Grandma to mess up something like this? Something this big?"

"Eli. No."

"I just need some time to think. I need…" I need to get into Grandma's head and figure this out. "I'll just stick around a little longer. It's almost Christmas anyway. The babies are due soon, and we need to go through some of the stuff in her bedroom to clean it out." I can't leave on this note. I wasn't here when Grandma died. She's trying to tell me something. She's trying to tell me something that she started telling me eleven years ago. Was that what Lara said?

"You're gonna stay until Christmas?" He can't seem to

hide the shock in his voice. "That's"—he checks the date on his smartwatch—"almost three weeks away, including Santa Day."

I look at my own watch. December sixth.

"Yeah, I'm staying until Christmas." I sigh. So much for my escape plan.

November, thirty years ago

I find Tommy in his bedroom, tears streaming down his cheeks in such rapid succession that I wonder if the streaks will be permanent. "Hey," I say and plop down on his bed. "Grandma is downstairs. She said it's time to go."

He sniffs and chokes on a sob. His tears don't stop, and somehow, I manage to make him cry even harder with that simple sentence. "I don't wanna go, Eli. I don't wanna leave Mom." He hiccups and flops back on his bed.

I don't know what to say. I'm not accustomed to comforting others. It's typically me receiving the consoling since Dad died almost two years ago. I glance around his empty room. He packed everything into a couple duffels and two boxes. Everything else is being auctioned off, and the house is being sold. I turn back to Tommy and shrug. "She's not even here, Tommy. She's in jail. We have to go with Grandma."

He buries his face deeper into the pillow and shakes his head. "Why did she do it?"

I wish I had an answer for him. The details have been kept a secret from us, so I don't know exactly how deep she went, but from the few conversations I've eavesdropped on, Mom was drinking too much and taking some pills and maybe something else. Tommy and I were both questioned. We're both being sent to live with Grandma.

"It's time to go," I repeat.

He sits up and looks at me. "Why aren't you sad?"

"She didn't die, Tommy. We're going to live with Grandma for a little bit. Mom will be back soon. She just needs some help dealing since Dad died. This isn't forever." I say it with more attitude than I intend to. I really don't see the problem. Mom said it's just for a little while, and she's going to get help. I believe her because when Dad died, I did weird stuff, too. I broke the head off my favorite Barbie, and I cut the hair of every other doll I owned. I stole money from Mom's change jar and hid pictures of my dad in the back of my closet. Mom never reprimanded me for any of it. She told me grief is complicated, and it makes us think and do things out of character because we're adjusting to a new life without someone we love. I trust Mom, so I know this is just temporary.

He shakes his head. "You're wrong, Eli. This is permanent. You're just too young. You don't know."

"You're not that much older than me."

"It doesn't matter. Trust me, we're done living with our parents forever."

I shrug. "Maybe." I play it nonchalant, but I'm scared he's right because I also trust Tommy. I don't want to be treated like a dumb kid, but I honestly don't always know what's going on. "I have basketball practice in an hour. We really need to go." He doesn't move, and I'm getting worked up. Youth basketball is the only distraction I have right now, and I hate being late for it. "Look," I say, softer, "Grandma is getting older and always needs help with things. Maybe this will be good for her."

He wipes his nose. "Yeah." He sighs and finally stands, slinging a bag over his shoulder. "She's really sad, too."

"Exactly. Just think of it that way. This isn't us losing our mom, it's us taking care of our grandma."

He hands me the other bag. "Right. We need to take care of Grandma."

CHAPTER THREE: THE OFFER

Tommy and I drove separately to Lara's office so fortunately, we don't have to keep bickering on the way home. I was planning to leave her office with a friendly handshake and a phone call to the trailer rental company I already had arrangements with to haul my new inheritance up north. I even had a driver lined up so I could peacefully follow in my sporty four-door all the way back to Minneapolis. Instead, I practically stomp out with my bottom lip protruding, only to lazily drive around town and avoid going home.

A humorless laugh erupts from my lips when I consider the *really* hilarious part of all of this: I don't know anything about cars. I'm not even remotely interested in vehicles or collecting anything mechanical. I just wanted something classic and pretty to call my own. It was always promised to me, and so I wanted it. We couldn't just "switch" like Tommy suggested. Not until I know why this happened. Eleven years ago was the last time Grandma made a change. I was in my late twenties. I had just been published and was starting to make some money. But what was she trying to tell an old version of me?

My phone vibrates in the cupholder. I slow to a stop at an intersection. I'm the only car in sight, so I shift into park and grab it. It's a text from Rae, my best friend and a damn good one to have. *Hey, girl, I'm thinking about you today. I have some exciting stuff to tell you, so get your ass back up here asap.*

I rub my eyes. If only she knew. If only I had the patience to explain via text. I type up a quick apology about not knowing when I'll be back. I tell her I'll call her later this week.

With a sigh, I shift the car into drive and flip the blinker to turn into Pump It, the lone gas station in town. Out-of-towners find the name hilarious and can occasionally be found on the side of the single highway that touches Maple Park, trying to take a picture of the illuminated sign. Having grown up here makes it difficult to see the sexual side to the name. It's just part of everyday life and routine, like a lot of things in a small town.

I don't need any gas, just a break from jittery driving. I put the car in park and tap my fingers on the wheel, contemplating if I really want to go inside.

"Just get a bottle of water," I instruct myself. "Water first. Talk to Tommy second." I nod with finality, deciding this is the process I need to digest everything that's happened in the past few days. "Okay," I whisper and kill the engine. I reach for the coat I borrowed from Grandma that has yet to grace my body. It's a bright yellow peacoat. A moving target. Something I wouldn't typically wear but something Grandma probably loved. She always liked to make a statement.

Aside from the random Christmas decorations, the inside of Pump It is just as it's always been. A few rows of snacks, candy, chips, and all the wonderfully overpriced bite-sized goodness one loves to see after filling their gas tanks. The back wall has all the sugary drinks, cold coffees, beer, and ice cream in the coolers. Warm coffee and tables line the far side near the public bathrooms. Retirees like to hang out here on weekday mornings to gossip about all the latest drama in town. I'm sure I've been the topic of conversation more than once.

I only get two steps inside the door, and I'm already distracted by the food warmer just off to the side of the cashier's counter. I breathe deeply in spite of myself, allowing the aroma to take over. I can practically feel the crunch of a deep-fried cheese ball in my mouth. Maybe I need something to eat, too.

I don't even turn to look at the cashier behind the counter before greeting her. "Hey, Harper."

"Holy shit, it's you," she says with a hint of jest in her voice.

I walk right past the warmer and turn toward the coolers. "Yeah, it's me," I say over my shoulder. I quickly find what I'm looking for and head back to the front.

"Just this?" she asks and doesn't make a move to scan the bottle.

I look up and realize she is waiting to make eye contact and smile. Harper was a year ahead of me in school, sandwiched right between Tommy and me. She's been working at Pump It since she was fourteen and will probably own the place someday. She's never been the type to grow beyond what's been placed in front of her. She graduated from school, kept the same job, and thrives off a constant state of ease.

I'm fairly certain Harper knew I was gay before I ever came out. We had one of those silent understandings about each other before it was so widely accepted. Aracely and I used to joke that Harper is a "hundred-footer" because we could tell she was queer from a hundred feet away. I've never known her to wear anything but flannel button-downs over graphic T-shirts. If she's not at work, she may also have a ball cap over her short, strawberry hair.

I used to suspect that she had a little bit of a crush on me, but I also used to think she had a crush on Tommy. It could be both. Could be neither. I'm not really sure of anything anymore.

I attempt to smile back, but I know I fall short.

She grabs the bottle to scan. "Sorry about your grandma."

"It's fine," I mumble. "Thanks." I tap my card and shake my head when she offers me a receipt.

As I turn to head out the door, she whispers that I should tell Tommy she's sorry, too. I wave in assent without looking back. "Are you staying for Santa Day?" She's attempting to make small talk, but I'm not in the mood.

"I don't know. Probably not," I lie. I just told Tommy I was staying. "I need to head out. Good seeing you." I step away, keeping my eyes on the floor. I only get one full step before I run right into someone with enough force to push an *oof* past my lips.

I reach out to stabilize the person and begin a string of Midwest apologies for taking up space near another human being. "Oh gosh, I'm so sorry, I didn't—"

"Eli."

I freeze and focus on the face of the person I nearly knocked over. "Cely. Hi."

Aracely smiles. "Cely, huh? Been a while since I've heard that." I'm not sure how it's possible, but it seems like her smile grows even wider as more teeth come into view, and a light shade of pink colors her cheeks.

"Yeah." I shake my head. "Sorry. I'm not with it today."

"Yeah," she echoes and squeezes my arm. "Nice coat." Her hand stays on my arm just a moment longer than necessary as she stares at the vibrant yellow.

I tilt my head at her in question when she meets my eyes.

"I bought this coat for Elisabeth last Christmas." My heart swells at the sentiment.

"Wow," Harper interjects. I honestly forgot she was behind the counter. "This is like déjà vu." She snorts and waves a lazy finger between Aracely and me. "You two…" She lets out a low whistle and doesn't bother to finish her thought. "Kinda like those two girls from your books, Eli."

I roll my eyes. "I gotta go. Thanks for the water, Harper." I step around Aracely. "And sorry I ran into you." I finish my former apology and shake my head at Harper. I push the door open and head quickly to my vehicle.

"Eli, wait." Aracely's voice follows me.

I stop before getting into the car and take a deep breath. I should have known I wouldn't get away so easily. I turn, and she's already so close I can touch her. I shiver, but I tell myself it's because of the cold and not her proximity. "Look, I'm sorry. I can't even string two words together right now. I'm in town until—"

She doesn't give me a moment to even consider what's about to happen as she gently slides her hand up the side of my face and tangles it in the hair behind my ear. She steps into me and guides me forward until our bodies are touching and she has one arm wrapped around my back.

My body remembers how to hug Aracely long before my brain catches up to what I'm doing.

I pull her hips closer and tilt my head to bury my nose in her thick hair. The move must surprise her because a small noise escapes her throat. She leans farther into me in a way that makes me fully relax as my arms tighten around her. I lose myself for a moment and melt into the embrace. I can smell the perfume from her shampoo. It transports me to a time that I've spent many years trying to heal from. This is dangerous territory.

After a short moment, someone walks past us and into Pump It, effectively breaking whatever trance we were in.

We pull apart, and she steps back.

My chest is heaving. "What was that for?"

She runs a shaky hand through her wavy hair. "Well, I was going to check on you because obviously you're not okay, and I just wanted to talk, but the closer I got to you, the more…I don't know. I think my brain just short-circuited, and I tried to comfort you in a way I used to."

I force out a breath of disbelief at what just happened. "I hope you didn't just hug-cheat on a girlfriend."

"Wife, actually," she replies so casually it nearly knocks me over. "Kidding. Oh God. That was a bad joke." She's nervous. So much so I can actually see her shaking.

I lick my lips, and a sense of calm washes over me, although I'm not exactly sure why. "Aracely, relax. It's fine."

She hides her face in her hands. "I can't believe I just said that. Or that I just…" She motions between our bodies. "This is not how I wanted this to go, Eli, you have to believe me. I honestly—"

I wave her off, feeling stupid for having forgotten her promise to fall out of love with me the day she broke up with me. "I get it. It's fine. Thanks for your condolences." I pull the door handle and slide behind the wheel, starting the car before she can respond. Out of my peripheral, I see her standing with her arms crossed, so unsure of herself. I know I should stay and comfort her. She lost someone, too.

Instead, I do what I've taught myself to do for the past two decades: run and hide.

❖

I could never, even from the wildest depths of my imagination, have believed I would be burying my grandma, blindsided by her will, and embraced by my ex all in the same day.

And there's still light in the sky. More opportunity for insanity as I drive aimlessly around my hometown, still avoiding going home and talking to my brother. I drive past the house Tommy and I lived in with our parents before everything went downhill. It's barely recognizable after going through more owners and various renovations. I'm grateful each owner had the good sense to keep the porch that covers the entire front and wraps around the side. The corner lot is a prime location to view two streets near the main section of town. I turn at that corner and see the large porch swing my dad built hanging at the far end. It looks like it could use a fresh coat of paint, but it's still a piece of him for the next family who lives there.

A sharp pang shoots through my chest. Dad's death had knocked our lives so far off course that I don't know if Tommy or I ever fully processed the trauma. He was young, and it was a shock that ran deep through a community that loved him so much. I rarely think about my father because I never wanted to think about the *what-ifs* had he not died. I was just a child, so it was fairly simple to put my time and energy into extracurricular activities and school. He was a motorcycle mechanic. He loved his wife, kids, church, hometown, and mother with everything in him. He was an avid football fan, especially college football, which was something neither Tommy nor I inherited. I think he was gone before he had a chance to spread his love of the game to us.

We used to put flowers by his headstone every year on his birthday, but I'm not sure if Tommy kept that up after I left. Occasionally, a memory of him will surface without warning, and I am crushed by how mournful I am that he never got to watch us grow up. I miss my dad, but truthfully, I don't have very many concrete memories of him. I think my brain buried them for me so I could heal.

I drink the last bit of my water, wishing it was filled with more flavor and alcohol, and turn down the next street that leads to the schools. As I near the high school, Pete exits through a side door and walks in the direction of what I assume is his truck. Before I can change my mind, I flip the blinker and turn into the lot. Pulling up next to him, I roll down the window. "You must be a really good principal if you're here this late."

He shields his eyes from the setting sun. "I don't like to be drowning in the mornings, and it's peaceful in the evenings. Quiet."

I hum awkwardly and look at my hands on the wheel. I didn't really have a reason for stopping to talk to him. I just wanted to distract myself.

When I don't say anything, he says, "You okay, Eli?"

"Yeah." I wave him off. "Yeah, just a long day."

"The service was nice."

"The meeting after wasn't."

"Oh?" He shuts his truck door and turns to me.

I put my own vehicle in park and motion to the passenger side. "Yeah, wanna get in and go for a drive? I'll tell you about it." We haven't spoken in years before the last two days, but he was the one who originally offered to hang out, and I'd love to talk to someone who isn't my brother.

"Yeah," he says eagerly. "Of course. How about we go to BJ's for a beer and some food?"

"Will your wife mind?"

"Nah, I'll call her on the way." He walks around the front of my car before I even have a chance to answer.

❖

BJ's is eerily the exact way I remember it. The same tattered barstools and exposed beams in the ceiling. I remember coming in after basketball games and ordering way too much fried food while hogging the pool tables. We were the epitome of annoying teenagers in an adult public space, but we didn't care.

Because of the season, there's an old tree in one corner decorated with a bunch of alcohol-themed ornaments and an obnoxious amount of string lights. I take notice of the mistletoe wrapped with purple ribbon that's hanging in the hallway by the bathrooms. As if I wasn't already on a nostalgia high, that one makes my head spin. I squint at the purple ribbon, the single piece that makes it recognizable. I was the one who wrapped it on there. I shake my head of the memory and follow Pete to an empty high-top.

Once we have beer in front of us, I spill everything so quickly I can barely get it out fast enough. I didn't pack my therapist, so an old friend will have to do. Pete's eyebrows are practically at his hairline as he nods along.

"Wait." He holds up a hand, silencing me mid-rant. "Aracely hugged you?"

"Pete, I said that, like, five minutes ago, keep up." I reach for another fried cheese ball and drown it in some ranch. I have been craving some since I saw them at Pump It.

"I know, I know." He shakes his head. "I just can't believe she finally found the courage."

"What do you mean?" I frown and take a long pull from my beer.

"Oh come on, Eli." His look is pointed. "You know that girl has always—"

"Wanted me naked?" I joke but regret it as the heat spreads from my ears to my cheeks.

He snorts. "Among other things."

"Like?" I take another drink to hide the waver in my voice at my sudden burst of nerves.

"Marry you."

I choke and cough as I slam the bottle back on the table. I shake my head. "She dumped me. Remember?" Not only dumped but also pushed me away and cut me out of her life so ruthlessly, I wasn't sure if I'd ever recover. And clearly, to some degree, I haven't.

"Fine, keep trying to deny it if that's your comfort zone." When I don't answer, he says, "What about other relationships? You been dating up there? Have a group of friends? Your life is such a mystery. You don't ever update any social media, and your family is very tight-lipped when it comes to you."

I pick at an imaginary spot on the table. I knew this was coming. "Yeah, I have a really good friend, Rae. We've been close since I moved up there, but now she's my attorney and handles all my paperwork and contracts for the books. It complicates the friendship sometimes."

"Nice. Is she an ex?"

I snort a laugh. "No, it's never been like that. I've dated, though. Lots. There was one serious one. I almost married her, but we had a falling-out at exactly the right moment to ruin everything."

"Ouch."

I shrug. "It wasn't meant to be."

He takes a large drink. "And basketball?" he asks quietly, as if not to upset the equilibrium. I know it's probably a weird topic, considering I took a full ride scholarship to play ball in Minnesota and then quit after my sophomore year.

I scrunch my face. "I was burnt-out. Didn't feel like there was much of a purpose for me on the team anymore." It's not a lie, but it's not the full truth. I crashed so deeply into a depression my first year of college that I was drinking too much, exercising too little, and never had my mind in the right headspace. I started hooking up with girls on the team my sophomore year, and it led to a lot of unnecessary drama. I knew I was at the center of it, and I had earned minimal playing time. I wasn't living up to my potential anyway, so I handed in my jersey at the end of the season and never looked back. I threw myself into writing and my classes, and it worked. Basketball was a chapter in my story but not my whole story.

He nods, accepting my answer. "Is writing your full-time job or do you have other things that occupy your time?"

"Am I being interviewed right now?"

He shakes his head. "Just genuinely interested. It's pretty obvious that my job and family are how I spend all of my time.

I come here"—he motions to the bar—"about once a month with some friends, but that's it."

"I actually do a side gig helping Rae with her boutique firm. It helps fill the empty minutes and clears my head to be organizing and tracking all her files and calendar."

"Like an assistant."

"Kind of, but with way more pull and none of the dirty work."

"Nice, she sounds like a good friend to have." He takes a long pull of his drink and knocks on the table. "Okay, back to Elisabeth's will."

I straighten. "Well"—I clear my throat—"that's pretty much it, actually. I haven't spoken to Tommy since we left Lara's office."

He leans forward slightly as I gesture to the server that I want another beer. "What are you going to do?"

I sigh exaggeratedly. "I don't know. I'm going to stick around Maple Park until Christmas, I guess."

"Great," he practically yells and looks around before lowering his voice. "I have a proposition for you."

"I *was* being interviewed," I accuse him.

He holds up his hands in surrender. "Just hear me out, okay? You can at least do that." He sticks out his bottom lip, and I hate myself for laughing at his antics.

"Fine, but I'm ordering more food."

After an over-explanation, an appetizer, and another beer each, Pete finally lands the plane on his grand plan, which is to have me work as a full-time substitute at the high school until the holiday break. "It would really help me out. The state waived all teaching requirements to be a sub. All one needs is a bachelor's degree and a pulse, and that's enough for me." He tips his beer at me.

"How appealing," I say with no emotion.

"I will literally beg you. I have teachers gone every day and classes uncovered. It pays decently well to essentially babysit." He motions to the server. "Plus—"

"Pete, I don't need the money," I start to explain and then stop. "Wait, plus what?"

"Well, I can't keep covering classes myself because I need to do some investigating. Rumors of a teacher-student relationship have been circling to the point it can't be ignored. I have some ideas but can't put anything together without more time." His face and tone are somber, and I can't imagine the weight he carries trying to keep a building full of other people's children safe and productive. It sounds like an impossible task. And now he may have a statutory rape case to deal with.

"That's why you were at the school," I say, finally connecting the dots.

"Yeah." He sighs. "I was reviewing counselor's notes from students who have been reporting what they've heard. We have a few social media posts, but they're so cryptic, I can't decipher them."

"Cryptic how?"

He shakes his head slowly. "I can't, sorry."

"Right. Yeah, I know that."

"Honestly, I don't know if anything has even happened or if it's just rumors. That's why I'm collecting information and trying to piece it together before I go accusing any adults or pressing students for answers." He looks a lot older than he did just a few minutes ago. This could really drag his reputation and ruin a career or a young life, depending on where the truth lies.

And now I find myself overcome by the need to help. He did drop everything to let me talk today. This is a chance to show how grateful I am. "Well, shit." I grunt, knowing what I'm about to say. "I can help you out. I'll sub for you. Just like babysitting, right?"

His eyes light up. "Really?"

"Yeah, and I can keep my ears open for any information that might need reporting. I mean, what else am I going to do while I'm in town?"

He grabs his chest in a dramatic fashion. "I appreciate this so much. I'm going to get your approval fast-tracked as much as possible to get you in by next week."

The server sets a beer in front of me, and I turn to her. "Just bring me another right away, please." I'm going to need to be drunk until Monday if I'm really about to do this.

❖

"You can't be serious." Tommy's voice reaches a volume I've never heard from him. "You're not going to help me sort this out at all? I have two babies on the way, Eli. I don't have time for this bullshit."

I pinch the bridge of my nose to repeat, yet again, what I've been trying to tell him. "Tommy. Listen. There is no way Grandma would mess this up. Can we please just coexist for a bit while I try to figure it out?" I sway slightly. I had four beers with Pete, but I don't want Tommy to know that, so I try to focus on keeping my balance steady.

"Coexist?" He scoffs. "You took a substitute teaching job at the high school. What is actually wrong with you? Are you having a midlife crisis or a complete mental breakdown? I can't even comprehend this right now."

"I only need to stick around for a couple weeks. You're acting like I'm a monster, but I'm not. I'm your sister. Our grandma died. My nephews will be here soon. Maybe I want to be here? Did you ever consider that?" I don't want to be here at all, but I know Tommy well enough to know it will tug at his heart.

He releases a long breath and looks at me, tears in his eyes. "I still don't understand why she did it. I have a lot going on right now, Eli. Grandma was really excited about the babies, and now she doesn't get to meet them. I wanted her to meet them." He chokes back a sob. "I'm overwhelmed. Just promise me you're not trying to take this house from me. I need it. I have kids."

"Tommy." My voice is barely above a whisper. "I'm not going to make you homeless with two kids. I wouldn't do that." Sibling love-hate relationships aside, I would never want to see him suffer. I truly want the best for him. We both came from the same trauma, so a victory for either of us is good for both of us.

"I really miss her." He wipes his eyes. "It feels like I've lost a piece of my body. It's weird she's not here, and I can't hear her moving around in the kitchen or laughing at the TV."

Until now, I hadn't fully considered how much time Tommy spent with our grandmother. He hasn't been without her since we were young. He's lost his companion. I want to say something smart to comfort him, but we're too far disconnected for it to be possible. I haven't been around Tommy in so long that I'm not sure how he even likes to be comforted anymore.

I'm starting to feel all the emotions bubbling to the surface again, and the desire to drunkenly rip through some really good carbohydrates fills me. I fidget with anticipation as I glance toward the kitchen, wondering what's left from the funeral food or the casseroles from all the neighbors. That may be one thing I miss while living in the city. I don't even know most of my neighbors' names, let alone bring them food.

"Eli, are you even listening to me?" Tommy's voice brings me back.

"No, sorry." I rub my face. I need to distract myself before the whirlwind of everything that's happened in the past couple days sinks me into a place I can't easily come out of. "What did you say?"

"How are you gonna handle Aracely?"

I frown, unsure what she has to do with any of this. Does he know she hugged me? I know this is a small town, but damn, if that news already made it to his ears, maybe I really am out of touch. "I'm not planning on seeing her again."

He blows his lips dramatically. "It'll be kind of difficult considering she's a teacher at the high school."

"What?" I practically spit. "Since when? Why? What subject?" I can't get the questions out fast enough.

He shrugs as if to say I'll have to find out on my own and walks to his bedroom.

"Pete." I bury my face in my hands. "You asshole."

June, twenty years ago

"Please don't do this," I cry into my hands. "Please." I'm begging now, but I can't help myself.

Aracely has a few stray tears running down her face, but she's frustratingly calm. She keeps repeating the same few sentences so robotically, it's like she spent the entire morning practicing them. "Eli, it's for the best."

"The best for who?" I repeat for the tenth time. "Please explain this better. Stop saying the same shit over and over. Why are you breaking up with me? I thought you loved me."

"I do." She sighs again. She sits next to me on the bed and takes my hand. It's the first time she's touched me since coming over this morning. She looks at the picture of us from Santa Day a year and a half earlier on my nightstand.

I put my hand on the side of her face and guide her eyes back to me. I press our foreheads together. "Baby, please don't do this," I whisper. "I love you. Whatever is wrong, we can fix it. I promise, *I* will fix it."

She sniffs and pulls me into her so tightly, I nearly lose my breath. "I love you so, so much, Eli." She pulls back and looks me in the eyes. "But I'm holding you back. You have to take that scholarship. You have to go."

Money. My resentment is rising. I attempt to latch on to some resolve and take a steadying breath. "Come with me," I beg. "It'll be fine. We can make this work."

She shakes her head. "I have a scholarship, too. I need to follow the money, just like you."

"Why is money more important than me?" I snap at her. "More important than us."

"You know that's not true," she bites back. "Don't do that." Her family never had it very easy. Her grandfather immigrated to Maple Park for a job opportunity, but it took years to find his way to financial security. Her mother had to do the same after being left a young single parent. They've come a long way, and it's not the case anymore, but I think the fear of financial ruin scares Aracely more than anything. While most kids were scared of monsters under the bed, Aracely was told stories of what it was like to not know where the next meal was coming from. She shared this part of her life with me in confidence that I would always be understanding and know it's a vulnerable spot for her.

Kind of how my parents are a tender area of my life, and I don't share much about them with anyone but her. "Long distance will work," I argue.

"It won't. I know you. You won't focus, and you'll drop out and come back."

She's not wrong. I won't leave without her. She is my future; I can feel it in my bones. As much as she's worried about money, I'm only worried about losing her. "Maybe I'm not meant to go."

"You are."

"Not if it means losing you." The tears are flowing down my cheeks as my voice breaks on the final word.

She hiccups through her own cry. "It's me or your future, and I won't take that away from you. I won't." She kisses my forehead. "I can't do that to you, Eli."

"Don't I have any say in this?" I pull away from her. "Look at us right now. How is this the best option?"

"Eli," she starts to say more, then stops. I can tell she's struggling to find the words to justify that breaking up with me is the right thing to do. She sucks in a long breath and straightens her shoulders, finding her nerve. "It would be stupid for either of us to compromise our futures right now. You know that." She looks at her hands. "We'd probably end up broken up eventually, and then we're screwed. You're going to fall out of love with me eventually anyway. We both will. I'm trying to save us from making a mistake."

Indignation boils inside me, and rage fills me to the brim. "Do you truly believe that?" I can't keep the shock and disdain out of my voice.

She remains quiet, looking at her hands.

"Seriously," I say louder. "Money is more important than us, and it's fine because we'll both just…move on?"

She doesn't move. I'm not sure if she's even breathing.

"I guess I was deeper in this than you were. I didn't realize we were just a fling." I choke on the words as a sob bubbles over.

She stands and walks to the door. "It's over, Eli. Sometimes, people need to let each other go."

"So our lives will be better if we're apart? That's what you're saying? Because if that's the case, sorry I wasted your time."

She wipes her eyes and shakes her head. "I know you're mad, but it's over. It's okay if you hate me."

"Just go, then," I say with more hate than I intend. "Have a nice life."

She manages a laugh, but it's filled with disbelief.

"Go. If I'm not worth the effort and money is more important, go." I grab the picture of us and slam it down with so much force, I think the glass cracks.

She accepts my push. "I'm going to my aunt's house in Kansas City for the rest of summer. I leave today."

I scoff and have to physically stop my jaw from dropping. "You were planning this. Dump me and then run and hide?"

She shrugs. "I'm not strong enough to be near you and follow through."

I look down and let the tears roll down my nose and chin. Finally breaking, I have no fight left. "Just go already. There's no coming back from this anyway. Go fall out of love with me and in love with someone else. I don't care."

She leaves without another word. Abandoned again. Nobody wants me. My dad died, and my mom left. I don't know why I'm surprised anymore.

I grab my phone from the nightstand to block and delete Aracely's number just as I hear the front door close. I toss my phone to the side and flop on my bed. Turning over and burying my face into the comforter, I scream as loud as I can.

A few moments later, I hear a soft knock on my door. I don't even have to respond to know it's Grandma checking on me. I'm sure she heard the entire conversation through the old floorboards. This house has never been good at keeping secrets.

"Eli?" Another soft knock. "Can I come in?"

I rub my nose and sniff. "Yeah," I barely manage to get out above a whisper.

The heavy wooden door creaks open on the rusted hinges. "Hi, honey." I hear her shuffle across the room and feel the dip of the bed once she's planted right next to me. "I saw Aracely leave in a hurry. Everything okay?"

I sit up to face her and wipe the tears from my cheeks. "She broke up with me."

She hums. "Did she say why?"

"She doesn't want to hold me back, and she doesn't want either of us to miss out on scholarships." I scoff at the ridiculousness of it. "So stupid." I shake my head and look at my hands in my lap. "She said I'll fall out of love, and it'll be fine."

Grandma runs her fingers through my hair and gently pushes it from my face. "It's not stupid. It sounds like she's making a very selfless decision."

My chest heaves. "I'm not stupid, Gram. I know that. But how can a selfless decision be the right choice if we're both miserable over it? It makes no sense."

"Aracely is looking forward. You're living in the present. Neither of you is wrong, you're just not compatible at the moment."

"Well, not being *compatible*," I say with as much attitude as possible, "is really screwing with everything we had planned."

She gives me a pointed look, then strokes my head again.

"Sometimes love isn't enough, darling. You can love someone with all your soul and still know you need to let them go."

"Love should be the thing that keeps us together."

She shakes her head. "There's a misconception about love. It's actually quite fragile."

I frown at her.

"Trust me." She smiles. "I've had a lot more time in this life than you. Love is fragile. It takes a lot of dedication and passion to keep the wheels turning. I think Aracely is seeing something different than you. She sees a person she loves and wants the best life for, but you see your best life as one with her."

"And I'm the one who's right."

"Possibly. Maybe you both need to grow separately to find your way back to each other."

"I don't want a future without her. I love her." I sob again.

"I know, sweetie, but she's made her decision. You must honor that."

I flop backward. "I'm not talking to her ever again."

"See? Fragile." She pats my leg. I feel the bed move as she gets up. "I'll give you some space. But remember, we make the hardest decisions for the people we love the most."

I pout, not ready to hear it as the door closes quietly.

A few weeks later, I pack my car and leave for college. My visits are short and few. I never add Aracely to any social media accounts, even when she requests me on every one of them as they become popular over the years. I never unblock her number, and I don't see or speak to her for nine years.

Excerpt from The Stone River Series by Eli Thomas

Book Two: The Oracle

The entity has an odd glow that illuminates the entire room in a purple hue. Joey takes a tentative step forward. Then another. The farther she gets into the facility, the clearer a shape comes into focus. Two more steps and she can make out that the entity is actually a woman.

The woman crouches in the middle of the floor, and it's clear her hands are restrained.

"Hello?" Joey calls out nervously.

The woman looks up and reveals deep yellow eyes. "Joey Abigail Campbell. Born 1960 to Paul and Alma Campbell. Named for her maternal grandfather. One sister, Mary. One niece, Abby, her namesake. High school counselor. Eleven lovers. Four relationships. Currently in love with Officer Si—"

"Wait," Joey cuts her off and holds up her hands in surrender. "Please, wait." She knows Sidney is somewhere in this building that's disguised as a cereal factory. She could be listening, for all Joey knows, and they haven't said those words yet. The woman stares at her and tilts her head. "What are you?" Joey asks in a whisper.

"A seer."

Realization floods Joey. This is tied to Mason's disappearance two years ago. All of this. The seance, the town curse, the alleged witches. "Do you know where Mason is?"

She nods.

Joey feels oddly comforted by her presence. Her body is

emanating warmth, and soft colors gently illuminate the air around her. "Where is he?"

"Come closer, dear."

Joey hesitates. "Are you one of the witches?" She easily recalls how it was to be possessed by Gelica, and that's not something she thinks she can survive twice.

The seer nods. "I am, but I am not like the witch who controlled you."

Joey chances a step forward. "I'm not going to hurt you."

"I know that, Joey."

"Right, of course you do." She stops just short. "What's your name?"

"My given name was Henrietta. My visionary name is Etta." Etta motions to her restrained hands with a thrust of her chin. "I will help you find the boy who partook in the seance, but I need you to free me from this prison."

"How do I know I can trust you?"

"Look inside yourself, Joey. I remind you of someone. Someone you trust. Someone who was mysterious yet loving. Someone who knew what was best for you, even when you didn't want to hear it."

Joey takes another step. "My grandmother."

CHAPTER FOUR: COMPLICATED

Pete somehow managed to pull some strings with a woman he knows at the state department of education to get my approval for substituting fast-tracked. So five days later, on a Monday morning, I find myself in a beat-up pair of black pants I manage to squeeze into and a gray quarter-zip. As I check myself out in the mirror, I have to chuckle at how much I actually look like a teacher. Especially with my computer bag slung over my shoulder. A tiny twinge of nerves settles in my stomach at the idea of having to be around youths and act like I know what I'm doing.

I pop my neck and straighten my shoulders. I've done way scarier things than this. Hell, I've spoken to semi-famous people. I've negotiated royalties with publishers. I've read excerpts of my own writing to rooms full of fans. I can handle teenagers.

Probably.

Maybe.

I allow myself a final once-over and head downstairs to say good-bye to Tommy for the day. I find him in the garage with the Starfire. "Hey," I press when I see a display of tools and parts scattered about. "What are you doing to the car?"

"Well, you decided to mess around with the house, so I guess I'm working on *my* car."

I roll my eyes. I had suggested painting one room. *One.* "Whatever, be a dick, then. I'm going to work."

"Have a good day, Ms. Thomas. Hope they drag your ass all the way back to Minneapolis."

"Screw you, Tommy. Shouldn't you be going to work? You have kids to support."

"Hasn't snowed in a while, business is slow. I'll be right here." He knocks on the hood of the car. Tommy has worked for the same lawn care company since he was sixteen. He's climbed up in status and rakes in a good paycheck three out of the four quarters of the year. His winters are fully dependent on snow patterns, so he's home more and has less money.

"Whatever," I jab and leave.

Not exactly the way I wanted to start my day, but we've been tiptoeing around each other since we were in Lara's office. I've been spending most of my time since seeing Pete avoiding people and feelings. I haven't come close to crying since the funeral, and it's almost becoming a problem. I can hear Tommy crying at night through the old floorboards, and I find myself actually *trying* to let a few tears out. I know I'm sad, but it's like my faucet was shut off, and all I'm doing is storing pent-up anger and sadness.

I attempted to sit and work on my book both Thursday and Friday, but it was no use. I reread the same chapters over and over again. I spent the better part of Friday afternoon debating if I needed the word "and" in a sentence I ended up deleting completely. On Saturday, I started going through Grandma's things and boxing up her clothes, shoes, and bathroom stuff. I didn't touch anything of value or anything sentimental, but Tommy came unglued when I suggested we paint the room. Apparently, at least that day, I had pushed too far.

❖

About thirty minutes after my bicker session with Tommy, I find myself walking into the main office of the high school I once attended. Immediately, I'm overwhelmed with regret. High school was a great experience for me, but there's a reason I moved on. This chapter is closed, and I have no desire to return.

Yet here I am.

The front office is pure chaos. It sounds like there are at least six phones ringing, but I can only see two. The two women who are somehow managing to answer every single one are just fielding them so quickly that the ringing doesn't stop. I stand there, dumbstruck, watching them easily take every call, greet each student who steps in, and answer questions from the school nurse as she pokes her head out from her office. It's when one of the women answers a phone and switches from English to Spanish like it's the most natural thing in the world that my brain short-circuits, and I turn to run. The education field is not the place for me. These people have skills beyond my own, and I will never compare. Just as I reach for the door, Pete spots me.

"Eli!" He comes sprinting out of his office. "Oh, thank you for coming. I was scared you wouldn't show. We have six teachers out today, and I need coverage." He steps up next to me and guides me to the desk of one of the women.

"Pete, this is insane. I can't do this." I motion to everything going on. Phones ringing, people talking, the door opening and closing and opening again and again.

"This?" He looks around like he doesn't even see the literal shit show right in front of him. I am truly amazed. "This is kind of a sleepy Monday, to be honest."

"It wasn't like this when we were young."

He laughs. "Yes, it was. You just didn't notice because you were a kid." He grabs a sub folder and key from behind the main desk area and motions to the doors leading to the commons area. "This way. You're going to be an art teacher today. I'll get you settled."

I follow him, still shell-shocked. He hands me the key and folder as we weave through students in the hallway. He delivers me to the exact same art room I took classes in two decades ago. The same Trojan mascot that was painted on the door before I even got to high school is still there, chipped and worn from the years, clearly with a few touch-ups, but still there regardless.

"Wow," I breathe, "déjà vu."

He unlocks the door and props it open with a wooden triangle block. "We've had a lot of updates around the building but no major reconstruction on this side. Some rooms are hopefully a little more modern than you remember." As we enter the classroom, Pete flips on the lights, and I jump in place, shocked to see two high schoolers making out.

"Seriously, guys?" Pete chastises. "Viktor, Anna, go to my office. I'll meet you down there in a few minutes."

Anna is a young Latina with shoulder-length dark hair. Her eyes are on the floor as she apologizes and practically runs past us. My bet is she's crying before she reaches the office.

Viktor, on the other hand, barely makes a move to stand from the table he's casually resting against. "Good morning, Mr. Kelley." He's pompous, and I already hate him. He also appears to be Latino but has a much lighter skin tone than either Pete or Anna. He slightly resembles Aracely, and that thought alone makes my throat tighten. I flash back to the hug in the Pump It parking lot and how nice it was to feel her so close to me.

"Viktor," Pete replies calmly. "I said I'll meet you in my office. How did you get in here, anyway?"

He stands and shrugs. "It was unlocked."

"Nice try. I know better." Pete points to the doorway. "Office."

Viktor walks up to me painfully slowly. "Hey, sub." He's standing too close for comfort, and regardless of him being a literal child, I find myself recoiling. I guess being a gross human doesn't discriminate with age.

"You're too close to me," I state flatly. "Go away."

He feigns shock and drops his jaw. "Mr. Kelley, did you hear that?"

"Go, Viktor. I mean it." Pete's tone leaves no room for negotiation.

Viktor holds up both hands in surrender and leaves the room.

"So, he's gross." I shudder. "How'd they get in?"

Pete snorts. "Come on. You know how."

I look around the room and spot the closet door. It's shared between the art room and one of the science rooms. It's a long, narrow space that allows for a lot of storage but has two entry points. Aracely and I made out in there once. We weren't as dumb as Viktor and Anna, I guess. I point to the door. "Science room."

He nods. "Ms. Clemens gets here extra early and leaves her door open while she makes her morning copies and coffee down in the office. Clever kids figure it out."

"Why did you ask him if you already knew?"

"I need to know what they know first." He takes a deep breath and motions to the room around him. "Okay, so art classes. I'll show you how to get logged in to our attendance as a substitute. Her lesson plans are on the desk, but really, just take it easy today, okay? Kids in these classes all have projects. They all know what they're doing. If you have any issues, text me, and I'll come running, I promise."

I swallow my quickly forming terror.

Pete walks me through everything and even scripts out the lesson plans on the whiteboard so the kids can just enter the room and read it for themselves. The teacher left a few names of "trusted students" for each class period so I can ask questions.

Pete leaves as the first bell rings, and I'm frozen in place. I can hear other teachers in the hallway greeting students as they enter. I remain seated and staring at the door with terrified eyes. As the first two kids enter the room and see a sub, they head to their desks without a word. I silently and weakly point to the instructions on the board. They both read and follow the instructions by getting out their current charcoal projects as others enter.

"Sub today," the taller of the two students calls out. "Get your charcoal projects."

They listen and continue to tell the others who arrive. I breathe a sigh of relief. "Can one of you help me take attendance when the tardy bell rings?" I ask quietly.

Immediately, there are three students walking toward me saying they'll do it. My shoulders relax. I can do this. I can teach.

About ten minutes into second period, I realize I am so, so very wrong.

Students start asking to go to the bathroom and never return. One boy makes a clay model of a penis and tries to jab other kids with it. A group of girls refuse to work on their projects and just roll their eyes when I gently prompt them. If kids aren't completely ignoring everything and playing on their phones, they're telling stories at obnoxious volumes and with such exaggerated lies, it astounds me. I overhear one boy telling his friends that he got out of a speeding ticket because a female cop wanted him so badly, she just couldn't help herself. I also found out who got drunk with who, who is sleeping with who, who is going to fight after school, and which teachers are "aight" and which are "sus."

By the afternoon, I'm exhausted and ready to leave. I'm completely checked out and just swiveling in my chair when Viktor walks into the room.

"Hey, sub." He pats his chest. "Remember me?" He turns to a buddy next to him. "She's the reason I have detention."

"You got yourself detention," I retaliate just as the tardy bell rings. "Please sit down and just follow the instructions on the board."

"Or what, sub?" he pushes.

"Just go away." I wave him off, my anger building.

He makes a kissing sound at me and backs off.

As I attempt to silently keep my composure, I notice a girl behind me near the teacher's desk. She's sorting papers and working quietly but clearly not a part of this particular class. She's young, but she isn't acting completely obnoxious or complaining nonstop. She's not even attempting to sneak her phone.

I feel like I should probably ask who she is or what she's up to, but the entire day has been such chaos that I can't find the energy to power through another conversation. For a moment, I wonder if she's a student teacher or a classroom aide. I take note of the Trojans hoodie and figure she's probably a student. Either way, she may be someone who can help me with the attendance for this class. I've been lucky enough to have someone help each period. That may be the one highlight of the day.

I roll my chair backward and knock on the table in front of her. The sorting pauses as she lifts her head and manages to freeze me to my very core with the force of her glare. My voice catches in my throat.

"What?" She enunciates the last letter like she's trying to spit poison at me. Definitely a student.

"Are you in this class?"

"No, I just sit in here for fun."

My jaw tightens. "Why are you sitting behind the desk?"

"I'm a student intern," she says and resumes her work.

"Oh." I shift awkwardly, slightly embarrassed. "Can you help me take attendance for this class?"

She scans the room. "Everyone's here."

I open the attendance on the computer and count the kids. Twelve kids are listed, but there are thirteen if I include her. "So where's your name?"

"That attendance is taken in a different spot." She finally stops her sorting and looks up at me.

"Can you show me?"

She makes a display of looking me over. It's judgmental and invasive to the point that I almost cower away. After some of the most uncomfortable seconds of my life, she must decide I'm worth her time. Her eyes soften a bit as she steps toward me. She nudges me to the side without asking permission and takes over the computer. Pulling up the attendance website, she logs in with ease. "See how there are multiple sections for this class period but labeled with different letters?" Her tone is condescending, but as long as she's doing this for me, I don't care. "That means there are more sections in one room."

She clicks open the session that has a single name listed. Ashley Amare.

"You're Ashley?"

She flattens me with a look that asks if I'm actually a complete idiot or just pretending to be stupid.

"Okay, okay." I hold up my hands. "Jesus, I was just asking."

"You're not a typical sub," she says flatly.

"Because I'm not a teacher," I say. I stretch my neck and check the clock. Thirty-eight more minutes of this day, but who's counting? I watch Ashley step back to her table to continue with whatever it is she's completing for the absent art teacher. "Why are you so angry?" I ask bluntly.

"That would be none of your business."

"Well, I opened the door. Make it my business."

"I'm not going to talk about my shit to a complete stranger." She looks around the room and back at me, almost like she's checking to make sure nobody is watching us. "Are you lonely or something? Why do you keep trying to talk to me?"

I roll my eyes despite knowing how childish it makes me seem. Outside of physical appearance, Ashley could be mistaken for an exact copy of me when I was eighteen. Brooding. Sarcastic. Kinda mean. Similar personalities is where our overlap ends. Her brown hair falls in loose curls past her shoulders and is complemented by her deep brown eyes. She's incredibly beautiful for such a young age.

Just then, Viktor decides to remind us that he is, in fact, still a garbage human being and stands way too close to me for the third time today. "Ignore Trashley," he instructs as he inches closer to the teacher's desk. "She's just pissed off because she loves someone who can't love her back."

The accusation sets off alarm bells in my head. This could be related to the thing Pete is investigating, but I certainly don't want this kid to be my source of information. I'm about to ask Viktor what he wants and why he dares to be this close to me *again* when Ashley responds from behind me.

"Eat shit, asshole."

Viktor's jaw drops in a fake dramatization. "Miss, did you hear that? Are you going to send her to the office?" He looks at me and points over my shoulder at her.

"No," I say simply, calmly. "You deserved it."

"*Wow.*" He draws out the vowel. "Guess you do have a special way with teachers, Ash. Too bad you can't fight your own battles." That line was meant to be a dig at her, but I don't miss the way his tone slightly shifts to one of jealousy.

"What do you want?" I snap my fingers in his face to bring his attention back to me. "Why are you up here?"

"I need to take a piss. Can I get a pass?" He stretches arrogantly and pats his own chest again.

I toss the pass book that's next to the sub plans at him. "Fill it out yourself. Just go."

He lazily writes his own pass and smirks at me. I'm sure he drew a penis or wrote something in reference to his penis so he could snap a picture and send it to his friends. I couldn't care less. I just want him away from me.

Once he's out the door, I turn back to Ashley. "Hey," I whisper.

Her eyes meet mine, and this time, the anger has subsided. She's trying to hide it, but she's hurt.

"You okay?" I ask.

She sizes me up again, probably trying to see if I'm even worth a response. A slow blink followed by a squint tells me she's made her decision. "I'm fine."

"Kids are assholes. I know it doesn't help at this moment, but life will beat him up eventually. He's a douche."

"You can't say that."

I shrug. "I'm not a real teacher, remember?"

A hint of amusement crosses her features as she rewards me with a genuine smile. Her face morphs into its true form, which is vastly different from the stoic girl who was staring at me only a moment before. Slight dimples pinch her cheeks as a mouthful of perfect teeth come into view. I can't stop myself from smiling back. I would tell her she has a smile so captivating, it could stop a person's heart, but she's had enough unwarranted attention for the day. It upsets me even more that paying her a genuine compliment was ruined because someone else was an idiot.

She breaks eye contact and looks back at her papers before I barely catch her response. "You're okay."

"Is that as close as you get to telling someone you don't hate them?" I ask when she looks up again.

"It is. Do I know you from somewhere? You look familiar."

My books are in the school library. My picture still hangs in the high school gym. Take your pick.

I shake my head. "Nah, I just have one of those faces."

❖

I swing by Pete's office at the end of the day. His head is in his hands as he's staring at paperwork scattered on his desk.

"Knock, knock," I say instead of actually completing the action.

His tired, bloodshot eyes come into view.

"Jesus, Pete. You okay?"

"No. But I'll figure it out. How was your first day subbing?"

"Being a teacher is genuinely terrible. I'm glad I never went into education."

He rubs his eyes. "Yeah. But will you please come back tomorrow? It'll really help me out."

"Yeah, I'll be here," I promise, even though I really don't want to. "I actually overheard something I think might be related to what you're investigating. The art teacher's student intern—"

"Ashley Amare?"

"Yes," I say quickly as he motions me into the room. "Wait, how did you know that?" I close the door and sit across from him. "Do you have all the interns memorized?" I would be thoroughly impressed but not surprised if he did.

He shakes his head. "That's the name that keeps coming up for me, too, so I have her schedule memorized. I just can't get myself to believe she's involved."

I frown and consider Ashley. From what little interaction we've had, I can't imagine she takes any shit from anybody. I also find it hard to believe she is even remotely interested in attention from an older teacher.

"I don't see it either," I say. "That one boy from this morning was teasing her. I feel like he's more of a suspect than her. He seems…weirdly jealous, I guess."

"Viktor." He sighs and scratches his chin.

"I think you have more information than I realized."

He snorts. "*You* have more information in one day than others have picked up on in weeks." He pushes a breath hard enough to motor his lips. "You're observant. Will you let me know if you hear or see anything else? Anything that seems like it might be important. Or not important. Shit, I'll take anything at this point. We can discuss this now since you're an employee with clearance and information."

"They're high schoolers, Pete. It's probably all rumors."

"Yeah, but what if it's not? I don't investigate one time and then…"

The answer hangs in the silence between us. One time he doesn't report it, and a child ends up hurt.

"All right, well, I'll leave you to it. I'll see you tomorrow."

I stand to go as he sighs. "Yeah, sounds good. And hey, thanks again. Seriously."

I walk out and quietly close his door so he can have some privacy. This place is far more depressing than I ever imagined.

When I get outside, I see Aracely waiting for me. She's perched on my car with her wavy locks blowing around her face. She smiles as I approach, and I try not to let it show how much her presence affects me. The one woman who can completely unravel me with just a look *would* age so gracefully that she's actually getting more attractive, that's just my luck.

"Hey," I offer with a frown.

"How was day one?" She slides off my hood and nudges me playfully. The gesture doesn't help the very little restraint I have when it comes to her. She's the only one who can completely unravel me with just a look. She puts a hand on my back, and I feel it all the way from my quickening heart to the intensifying arousal coursing through my lower body. How is it possible I'm still *this* attracted to her?

I move away and don't miss the way her face falls. "It was fine."

"That's great." She folds her hands in front of her. "Will I see you tomorrow?"

"Yeah, I'll be here." I unlock the door and open it to toss my bag inside.

"I'll bring us some lattes from Alma's," she offers. Alma's Coffee Shop has been a staple of the main street in Maple Park for as long as I can remember. Alma, who has never looked her true age, has been running the tiny coffee place with minimal employees since its inception. She says it keeps her young. Maybe that's why a woman who must be well into her fifties, possibly sixties, now looks younger and more vivacious than people two or three decades her junior.

"No, thanks," I say quickly, even though my mouth is watering at the idea of Alma's. This is dangerous territory. Aracely wants to make amends. Be friends. I want one of two things: to get her naked or to never see her again. It's a battle of my mind and my libido. I don't dare to allow my heart to enter this fight.

"Oh come on," she presses. "I know you miss it. Why else would you put Alma in your books?"

That makes me pause. "I didn't."

Aracely doesn't move. "You did." She waves in front of my face as if to wake me up. "Alma is Joey's grandmother. She's linked to the oracle because of her grandmother's roots. It's clearly an homage to your grandma and to Alma. There are quite a few references in there."

"I don't know why everybody keeps saying that." I nervously scratch the back of my head even though it doesn't itch. I recognize that I put a little bit of myself into the story, but clearly, there was more than I realized.

"No thanks on the latte." I open the driver's side door and slide past her to get in.

"Eli..." She sighs. There's no aggravation in her tone, just exasperation that I won't let her in.

"Cely, what do you want from me?" I throw my arms up and bring them down on the wheel. I've reached my limit for the day, and now my hurt and confusion from the past week is starting to boil over.

"How about just a conversation without our guards up?" She suggests it with nothing but genuine care.

I shake my head. "You were the one who wanted it this way, remember?"

I shut the door before she can protest. She steps back as I turn the key and bring the engine to life. I can just barely make out her muffled "Please just talk to me," over the sound of my music as I put the car in reverse and leave.

❖

On Tuesday, my nephews are born fourteen hours apart. Tommy left in a full panic on Monday night because Tara called and said she was heading to the hospital. About three hours later, he called me while completely spinning out because Angie had also gone to the hospital and was already almost fully dilated.

I woke up to the news that Angie had given birth to Otis just past midnight. Later in the day, in the final hour of playing the part of math teacher, I find out Tara has delivered Niko.

Tommy is over the moon. He can't stop crying and promises me I can meet them in a couple days after everything settles down.

I wish I could cry as easily as he can.

Otherwise, the second day of subbing is rather unspectacular. There is a teacher's aide or co-teacher in nearly every class. It helps tremendously having those second and sometimes third adults in the room.

The third day, however, is literal shit.

I'm being moved from room to room, wherever they need coverage. I don't see Pete all day, and I am repeatedly told he's in some admin meeting. I have to break up two verbal fights and dodge a fistfight in the hallway. I don't even bother to stop it.

I'm called a bitch, a snitch, crusty, sus, mid, and a pick me girl. I'm not entirely certain what most of those mean, but I don't care enough to ask, either.

I see Ashley near the end of the day. She rolls her eyes when I try to say hi while passing her in the hallway.

Aracely gives me a sad smile when we walk past each other to the bathroom. She shrugs as if to say, some days are just like this.

I don't have a chance to catch my breath, sit, cry, eat, or anything.

By the time I get home, I am beyond relieved *again* that I'm not actually a teacher, and I can leave this profession in the dust. It's thankless on so many levels, and I should win an Oscar for my performance of "caring adult." I could give two shits about these undeveloped assholes.

Just as I am about to down my second beer, my phone dings with a notification that there's an open sub position for tomorrow. I accept the job and toss my phone to the side before I collapse on the couch.

❖

On my way out the door after spending Thursday back in the comfort of the math classroom, a stray basketball rolls through the propped open gym door.

I stop the ball with my foot and roll it backward so my toe can slide underneath, and I kick it up just enough to start dribbling. After a few bounces, I cradle the ball under my elbow and walk into the gym to hand it back to whoever is in there.

"Never lost those skills, I see," Aracely says from behind me.

I jump at her voice. "Are you following me?" I mean it as a dig, but it comes out flirty.

"Just on my way home and was mesmerized by those dribbling moves."

"Stop it." I roll my eyes and turn back to the gym, but as I enter, it's empty. I can hear Aracely's steps behind me, and I turn with a frown.

"I think the girls just finished practice," she offers. "I'm sure it just rolled away, and none of them bothered to chase it." She points toward the locker room right as a loud barrage of laughter pours out.

I hum in acknowledgment. "Do you know where the balls go? I can put it away."

"Yeah, the same closet as always. Don't tell me the great Eli Thomas has forgotten her basketball stardom roots?" She presses a hand to her chest and drops her jaw.

"Don't be dramatic. I just didn't know if there was a new closet or addition or something."

She snorts. "Yeah, right."

I heave a sigh and turn to walk to the utility closet.

"Hey, wait." She jogs up behind me. "Are you in a rush? We could play a quick game of PIG."

I desperately try to stop the smile that pulls at the corners of my lips. "You mean, you could lose a quick game of PIG?"

"There she is." Aracely winks, and despite my best efforts, it makes my stomach drop in a satisfying way.

I let my bag fall from my shoulder and dribble to the nearest hoop. "I'll give you first shot." I turn and lazily toss her the ball.

"Don't take pity on me. I've kept up with my game. I play an adult pickup game once a week at the park."

"Ooh." I wave my hands dramatically. "Brag about it."

She comes to a stop at the top of the key and shoots without another word. The ball banks in, and she follows her shot to get the ball back to me.

I release a low whistle. "Well, well. Pickup games for the win. You always had decent form."

I walk to the place she shot from and shoot. The ball swooshes through the net. I chase it and throw it back to her.

She goes slightly left of where she catches it and shoots. The ball bounces off the rim. "Shit."

"It's over now, Hernandez," I tease.

Aracely retrieves the ball and tosses it back to me. Without hesitation, I set my feet and shoot off the pass, sinking the ball through the bottom of the net.

"You're such a show-off. You'd think someone who was an all-state athlete would have a little humility."

A laugh bursts from me as she shoots from my spot. "Have you forgotten everything? I'm not humble." The ball bounces off the rim again. "P," I announce.

She smirks to let me know she's not angry. "Don't feed me that 'I'm not humble' bullshit when you threw the state championship game to the Foster girl."

I sink another shot. "No, I didn't. You know that."

She dribbles the ball up to my spot and shoots, making it with ease. "Prove it."

I sigh and chase the ball. I pick it up at a weird angle off court and slightly behind the basket. I shoot up and over the backboard. Swish. "It's like that movie you love so much. The one about women playing baseball."

Aracely brings the ball back to where I shot and groans when she sees the angle. She sets her feet and misses.

"I."

As I go for the ball and try to decide where my final shot should be, Aracely follows me. "Okay, how is it like the movie? Would you just pick a spot?"

"It has to be where I'm feeling it. It's a process." I keep dribbling and looking at the hoop, trying to get a feel for where I can easily make it but also make it difficult for her. "And, yeah, at the end of the movie where the sister drops the ball."

"Exactly. She does it on purpose, so you're proving my point."

I click my tongue. "No, no, no. The younger sister finally outplayed her. Dottie was too competitive to do such a thing."

"She smiled at the end," she offers by way of explanation.

"Because she was proud of her sister. She was happy for her to have her moment. Don't discount Kit's character growth by saying it was just handed to her by her older sister. Sheesh." I finally stop at the free throw line. This is it. "Eyes closed," I call. I set my feet, dribble twice, twist bounce the ball back to myself and line my hands. I bend my knees and test out my stance. My eyes drift shut right as I push taller, arms in the air, flicking my wrist. I feel the ball roll off the tips of my fingers, and I don't even have to open my eyes to know it's going in.

Aracely grunts. "Jesus."

I hear the ball hit the floor and keep my eyes closed. "Did it go in?" I smirk, knowing damn well it did.

She bumps my hip with her own. "Move it. It's my turn."

I finally open my eyes with a laugh.

"Okay." She sighs and dribbles a few times. "Eyes closed." She closes her eyes and launches the ball.

Honestly, it was closer than her last shot but still a miss. "G."

"Fine, you win. But I still think the sister dropped the ball on purpose, and you missed that shot because you're a good human being. You may not have intended to on the surface, but deep down, a piece of you knew the Foster family needed the win more than you did."

Not bothering to chase the ball, I sigh and shrug. "I guess neither of us will ever know the actual truth. State runner-up still got us a trophy. I was honestly more disappointed we didn't make it back the next year."

"Don't remind me. That season was awful." She looks around thoughtfully, then back at me. "This is nice"—she motions between us—"going down memory lane with you."

I can't deny that she is at least a little bit right. "Yeah, it's not so bad. It's like…giving me closure."

"Do you need closure?"

I walk to where I dropped my bag. "Yeah, don't you? It's hard not to look back and wonder what path my life could have taken if I had made different choices."

"Like dating a boy instead of hooking up with me in the girls' locker room?"

"That I don't need closure on," I say with the utmost seriousness. "I would never wish to change that part." There's a comfortable silence while I stare at my shoes and try to muster the courage to ask something I've been wondering. "I have been meaning to ask you," I start softly, carefully. "About why you're here. I didn't realize you were even living back home, and then I found out you're working at the school…" I trail off and wait for her to respond in some way. When she doesn't, I say, "It just seems—"

"Out of character?"

"Yeah," I agree, grateful she finally said something. "I don't know. It's just not what I expected."

"You think I'm a sad failure."

"I would never say that."

"My mom got sick."

"Oh."

"Yeah," she says sadly. "So I decided to come home for a few years. I worked out a conditional thing with Pete for the family and consumer science position, kind of like you did, while I took teaching classes at nights and on weekends. I'm actually a licensed teacher now." She laughs at herself. "I never thought that would happen. Anyway, before I realized it, four years had passed, and Mom was in remission, but I just…never left. Now, six years have passed, and right when I was exploring other options and taking steps toward them, my ex-girlfriend shows up. Life is funny that way."

I resist the urge to ask her what those other options are as I sling my bag over my shoulder. My phone flies out of the side pocket, and starts to vibrate the second it hits the floor. Tommy is calling, but I silence it as I pick it up. "Aracely, I—"

She waves me off. "I know you're not staying, or you're not interested in being friends, or whatever excuse it is you're about to give me."

"It's not an excuse," I say. "We're not—" I'm cut off by my phone ringing again. Tommy. I grunt in frustration and slide my thumb over the screen to answer. "I'm on my way, Tommy." It comes out too harsh, and I know it. I'm going to have to apologize to him later. I hang up and turn back to Aracely.

"How's he doing with the babies?"

"He's fine. He wants me to come meet them, so I better…" I point my thumb over my shoulder.

"Yeah, of course. Tell him congratulations." Her face falls. She wasn't ready for our conversation to be over. Honestly, neither was I because it feels like we're finally clearing the air in some way. Maybe if I actually do find the closure I was talking about, I can move on for good. Maybe if I knew with finality that she did, in fact, fall out of love with me like she promised, we both would.

It'll have to wait, though. I have to get to Tommy.

❖

I don't go to the school on Friday. I tell Pete I'm not feeling up to it and attempt to deep clean the entire house instead. I clean the bathrooms, kitchen, and floors before I lose interest. I look through

Grandma's old picture albums, hoping it will bring out some tears. No such luck.

So I sleep. I sleep for over twelve hours.

I wake up, go to the bathroom, eat some food, and sleep some more.

Grief is complicated.

February, twenty-one years ago

The roar of a small but mighty crowd and the smell of buttery popcorn fills the air in the downtown arena. This isn't just any game. It is *the* game. We're playing for our school's first state title in girls' basketball. As a junior, I'm having the best season imaginable. I'm not sure if it's just blind confidence or actual skill coming from all the extra work I put in outside of the season, but I can't miss a shot. I don't only lead the team in points, I lead the entire conference, and I'm top five in the whole state. Teams don't dare foul me because I can sink free throws with my eyes closed.

Today is different, though. I'm not the star, and for the first time all season, exactly zero of the attention is on me. There's a girl on the opposing team who has been heavily covered by the news outlets for the past week.

Jeanette Foster.

She's also an all-state athlete and basically has all the same accolades I do. There's one huge difference, though. Her mom is one of the assistant coaches and was diagnosed with liver cancer near the beginning of the season. Her timeline is short.

The team has armbands that read "For Coach Foster" and have worn them all season. Jeanette's armband says "For Mom." Coach Foster has somehow managed to be on the bench for this game, cheering on her daughter for the title.

When it comes down to the last few seconds of the game and we're down by two, Jeanette has a moment no athlete wants at such a crucial time. Fearful and frantic, she impulsively fouls me at the buzzer, giving me two shots and a chance to tie the game to take us into overtime. If there's an overtime, we'll win. The momentum has been in our favor since halftime, and the only chant that can be heard from the crowd is the repetition of "Let's go Trojans!" We've come back from a twelve-point deficit. Foster's team is gassed, and mine continues to pick up the pace. Aside from my own performance, Tara Matthews can't seem to miss. I've had eight assists to her in the second half alone. Aracely has managed to get double-digit rebounds, and her long arms can get me the ball from almost any coverage.

As I take my position at the free throw line, I hear a sob from Jeanette near the opposing team's bench. I don't look. I shoot and easily sink the first shot.

There's another loud cry, and I make my own impulsive mistake.

I look at her.

She's hugging her mom and repeating, "I'm sorry," over and over again.

I know what it's like to lose a parent. I also know she's outplayed me this entire game. All her stats are higher, and all her shots are falling. If she loses this game, she will always look back at this moment. The moment she made a careless error. If my team wins, I would be considered the hero and the one who saved us, even if I wasn't the better player.

Jeanette's situation sinks past my heart and settles in my bones. I've played ruthlessly all season and have never given a single thought to anyone on any opposing team.

I dribble the ball and look at Jeanette again.

Her mom is going to die. Soon.

My dad died, and my mom left. I've been where she is.

Jeanette grips her mom's shirt in balled fists and continues to cry. Those tears aren't for this game. It's not about basketball at all.

I crane my neck and glance at Aracely. My girlfriend. After this game, no matter the outcome, I still have her. She will kiss me and tell me how much she cares about me, and I won't have to worry about losing her after this. I can't help but wonder if Jeanette has a boyfriend or girlfriend who will make her feel that way.

Or if she has a grandma to tell her that the only way out of her grief is through it, like mine told me.

I turn back to the hoop and shake my head. I dribble and clear my throat. I spin the ball in my hands and shoot.

When it comes off my fingertips, I think it's going in.

The ball bounces off the rim.

It's the only free throw I missed all season.

The opposing side erupts as my teammates fall to the floor in disbelief, Aracely being one of them. I let them down. I let her down.

Tara is sobbing so loudly about how it's her last game, it's all I can hear. Normally, I'd be rolling my eyes at her antics, but all I feel is numb.

I stand and stare at the basket until Aracely manages to stand, tears streaming down her face, and comes to get me. She walks me through the line to shake hands. When I get to Jeanette, I hug her. I'm not sure why, but it makes the camera clicks and flashes go wild.

A couple days later, that's the picture used by a *Des Moines Register* sports journalist on the front page. Jeanette and I are applauded for our amazing sportsmanship and how "Iowa Nice" has been ingrained into homegrown athletes. They interview me for the article, but all I say is I respect the way Jeanette plays, and she deserved the win. I'm asked at least a hundred times by journalists, coaches, teammates, friends, and family if I missed the shot on purpose. I always say no. Jeanette outplayed me. It's that simple.

Coach Foster dies eight days after Jeanette graduates. The *Register* does another article on the mother-daughter duo and a tribute to Coach Foster that summer. I am not mentioned once in the article, and it's better that way.

Grandma catches me reading it on the day it's published as I'm sunbathing in the backyard. "So sad to hear about that coach. She was very young. I'm sure her daughter is hurting."

"Yeah," I agree and fold the paper. "I know how that feels." I adjust my sunglasses and turn my face to the sun.

Grandma pulls a lawn chair up and sits next to me. "Mind if I join you? The sun feels nice today."

"Sure. Better get some sunblock for those pasty legs."

Her foot nudges my side. "You're rotten."

I laugh but don't open my eyes or turn my head.

"I'm proud of you," she says after a quiet moment.

I frown, open my eyes, and turn to her. "For what?"

"I know you didn't miss that shot on purpose. You genuinely played against that girl, and she won. You handled this whole thing with such grace. I'm just so very proud you're my granddaughter."

"Everybody else thinks I did it on purpose. Tara is waging an all-out war on me."

"Who cares what they think? Tara thought she was the superstar of the team. I'm sure it hasn't been easy that she got so little attention this season. Basketball isn't your entire future anyway. It might be part of it, but you're definitely a writer." She heaves a sigh the way she does before she's about to be arrogant. "You get it from me."

"Is that so?" I smile. "Have you finished that poem yet?" She was bragging about being the first true writer in the family a few weeks ago, so I challenged her to prove it by writing a poem.

"In fact"—she pulls a piece of paper from her pocket—"I did."

"No way." I sit up and push my sunglasses to my forehead. "Let's hear it."

"It's called 'When I Die.'"

"Grandma!"

"I'm getting old, sweetie, it's bound to happen eventually. Plus, I've found that if you accept that life will someday end and actually talk about it, it takes away some of its power."

"Whatever, morbid. Just read the poem."

She straightens her shoulders and reads:

When I'm gone from the world and there is no me,
Please place a bench with my name near the water
So people can come to visit and sit and just be.
But that's not where I want my ashes
Lean in and please listen carefully.

I need to be spread in all the beautiful places:
Mountains, oceans, lakes, and my backyard tree
I want to be where I was happy and felt loved
Because that's the perfect place to spend eternity.
If you're sad that I'm gone from this world
And I have no grave to come and see
Just close your eyes, feel the wind upon your face
Open your mouth, there I am, that dirt you taste is me.

I giggle and she shushes me. "Sorry," I whisper. "Keep going."
She looks back at her paper and continues:

I'm here when you hear a certain song
Or when someone quotes a movie line.
I'm somewhere bobbing my head along
And quoting back in perfect time.
Please smile when someone lets profanity fly
Or a sarcastic comment is said at the wrong time.
People laugh at inappropriate, here's why:
We all need a break sometimes, it's fine.

I smile at her. Just last week, she let the F-word slip out during dinner. Tommy and I gasped and feigned shock. I put my hand to my heart and chastised her the way she does to us when we curse. We all know she can swear with the best of them.
She looks back to her paper and continues.

Please save all thoughts and prayers
For someone more deserving than me.
Instead, plant something beautiful
And then give it away for free.
I want everyone to know that I loved my life
I enjoyed the adventure, the triumphs,
And even all of the hurt and pain.
It was a challenge at every step and
Given the chance, it's here I'd remain.

She gently bows her head at me and folds the piece of paper up. "Well, what do you think?"

"It was funny, yet deep. Your rhyme scheme could use a little work. There was a cadence to it, but it was uneven by the end." I tap my chin and hum as if I'm trying to think of more.

Grandma laughs. "You liked it."

"I did."

"Told you you're not the only writer."

"I'll make sure it's printed in your obituary someday."

"Deal. And I'll make sure to send you a list of constructive criticism about your first novel."

"Deal."

CHAPTER FIVE: TRADITIONS

Three single parents were created from Tommy's whole ordeal. I haven't asked if they need any help. I'm just assuming there are other family members helping both Old Angie and superstar Tara Matthews, who Tommy assures me has forgiven me for missing that shot. He told me to quit living in the past. I find it hilarious since I'm the only one who has actually moved on from this place.

Tommy tells me he's bringing each of the babies home for at least one night next week so the moms can sleep. One baby is formula fed, and the other is being breastfed, and he said the mom who is breastfeeding needs a week before she can pump. I honestly have no clue what any of it means, and I can't keep the details about which baby gets what straight. I know one of the boys is half-Black and the other is one-quarter Korean. Tommy definitely doesn't discriminate in his affairs, I'll give him that.

I was fully planning on hiding out in my old bedroom for most of their time here, maybe going downstairs for a few baby squeezes. Then, out of nowhere, Tommy offers for the two of us to take both babies at the same time on a Saturday morning so their moms can go Christmas shopping together.

As one infant screams from my arms in the direction of the second screaming infant in Tommy's, very unhealthy amounts of rage are seeping from my body and in the direction of my brother. "This isn't how I wanted to spend my Saturday, you dick!"

"Eli," he says, barely loud enough for me to hear, "screaming isn't going to make them stop crying." He flips the baby in his arms into an upright position and begins bouncing and patting his back. After a few shushes and there-theres, I follow suit.

Slowly, the baby in my arms starts to calm. Tommy has Niko pretty much silent just as Otis's cries slow, and a burp escapes his tiny body. I feel him relax, and then a small coo comes out against my neck as he snuggles in and falls asleep almost instantly.

I finally let out the air I have been tensely holding.

"Should we lay them down in the bassinets?" Tommy whispers.

"If you so much as move that baby even one inch, I will kick your balls so far up into your body, you won't need to worry about condoms again," I scream-whisper back.

"Let's just sit in the recliners." He tosses his head in the direction of the living room. We make our way slowly and both sit opposite each other, Tommy in his usual chair and me in Grandma's. I hold my breath again as I lower my body, willing the old thing to not squeak and wake this tiny child.

Once I'm settled without a noise from the chair, I release a slow breath of relief and start to rock and rub Otis's back. He already has Angie's feathery dark hair. I glance over at Tommy going through the same motions with Niko. He drops his nose to the top of Niko's head and smells him, smiles, and then kisses him. That must be the essence of parenthood. He's frustrated, sleep-deprived, lost, and yet, the happiest I've ever seen him. What a strange bond.

I smell Otis's head. Oh. Oh, I get it now. He smells fresh and a little like soft shampoo. The world hasn't beat him up enough yet to make him smell like dirt and depression. I breathe in the scent again and kiss his head the way Tommy did to Niko. I can finally feel my body relax. We haven't even turned on any lights in the house or opened the shades. Only the lights from the Christmas tree are illuminating the dark room.

I look over and see Tommy staring at me.

"What?" I loudly whisper.

"Do you want kids?"

"No, I think you're overpopulating the earth enough for the both of us."

"I want, like, six more. I mean, look at these two. It's amazing."

"Gross, Tommy. People with that many kids are gross. Their houses are dirty. They never have money or time to truly take care of their own kids."

"You are seriously a cynical bitch."

"Which of the baby mamas are you planning on having more kids with? Or is there another one waiting in the wings?"

"Well, I don't plan on being like that. But I don't think it'll work out with Angie or Tara, either."

"Ah, so they're gay."

"Would you shut up?" he practically growls at me. "They're not gay."

Tommy has had multiple ex-girlfriends move on from him and into relationships with other women. Most of them came out as either gay or bisexual shortly after. "Tommy, you have this wonderful, magical ability to make women realize their true selves. Don't squander that. Please, continue to sire children and make all the hot moms discover their true sexuality. In fact, find one for me, please. How many have there been? Four? Well, six after these two."

He points a threatening finger in my direction. "Don't talk like that in front of my kids."

I laugh quietly. We sit in silence for a moment, the only sound is the slight squeaking of the recliners in tandem. "So they're *shopping* together, huh?"

"Stop."

"Seriously, think about how easy that would make your life. I mean, as easy as it gets for a parent with multiple children with multiple people. Your baby mamas would get along. Your sons will live in the same home and see you on the same weekends. I mean, it's not breaking your heart or anything, right? You don't love either of them."

"I mean...it wouldn't be the worst thing, I guess."

"I always kind of thought Tara was a little gay anyway."

"Me too." He laughs and adjusts Niko to the other side of his body.

A few hours later, both moms show up at the same time to collect their infants. I waggle my eyebrows at Tommy as they bounce the boys at each other. I mouth the word "love" and point between them.

He flips me off.

Tara shifts Niko and looks at me. "Been a while, Thomas. How have you been?"

"Good," I lie. "You?" I ask out of trained behavior.

"Well…" She smiles at the baby. "Happiest I've ever been, actually." She beams, and despite my cynicism about all these single parents, they seem so elated. "I liked your books, by the way."

"Oh." I'm taken aback. I hadn't actually expected her to read them. "Thank you."

"Me too," Angie chimes in. "I've read them twice. I can't wait for the final installment. Don't suppose you'll give any spoilers?" She giggles at an annoyingly high pitch, and I am very quickly reminded why Angie and I never hung out outside play practices.

"Sorry, Old Angie, you'll have to wait until next September." I catch a waver in my own voice and briefly wonder if the rest of them heard it. Nerves. I don't have an ending, and my book is due to my editor for our first pass in less than a month. The more people ask about it, the more amped up I feel about the impending date.

"Old Angie?" Tara asks.

She shrugs. "She's called me that since we did theater together."

"Oh right, I forgot you had a foot in both sports and fine arts, Thomas. So well-rounded. No wonder you've done well for yourself."

I consider that statement. Have I done well for myself? I have a few friends, but only one true one. No girlfriend. An unfinished book. And a house I don't want. Isn't this what I've always wanted? People to see me as a success? I'm not so sure anymore, and I don't have Grandma here to talk me through it. "Thanks. Good seeing you both."

After Tommy makes promises to both of them he'll be by later tonight to help, they leave us in a very comfortable and welcome silence.

I release a long, exaggerated breath. I'm anxious about writing.

Sad that my grandma is dead. And now I need a distraction. "Well, I think I'm going to paint one of the rooms upstairs. I was also looking at the floors, and I think we can replace almost all of them for a reasonable price if I do most of the labor myself."

Tommy stares at me.

"And the light fixtures could use some updating." I turn and point. "And counters and cupboards in the kitchen. I know we need new windows, but I'll have to hire it done. There's a long list of everything I want to update on the outside, too. Like add a carport to the side of the garage and power wash the siding. With all of it, I'll probably be staying through the spring and into summer. I kind of want to see my nephews while they're still tolerable babies and not asshole children. So…why are you just staring at me?"

He rolls his eyes. "This isn't your house, Eli. Why are you updating it so much?"

"Resale value."

He points a threatening finger at me. "Don't."

"Relax. I'm kidding. Look, I have the money. I own the property, for now anyway, and I want to make it nice."

"Then I'm going to restore the Starfire."

"Good. Do it."

"And keep it."

"Why?"

"Because that's exactly what you're going to do to me, Eli. You said you're joking, but you're not. This is going to become one of your new passion projects. Flipping houses and selling for a profit. I can already see the stupid gleam in your eyes."

"Jesus, Tommy."

"Don't." He puts a hand up to stop me from responding any further. "Just don't." He stomps off to the garage and makes a show of slamming the door behind him.

Not about to let him get under my skin, I head to the basement to retrieve the paint.

❖

I'm about an hour into taping off, laying plastic, and painting one of the spare rooms when I hear a light knock. I turn to see Aracely resting casually against the door frame. She has a blue flannel shirt layered over a black tank that is hugging her in all the right ways. For a moment, I almost forget myself and give in to the urge to peel that flannel off with my teeth.

"Hi," she says with such a breathy tone I nearly faint. Maybe it's the paint fumes, or maybe it's because I still have an overwhelming desire to see her naked.

"Um," I stutter. "Hi."

She must sense that her presence has thrown me off balance as she raises a single eyebrow. "You okay?"

"Uh, yeah. Wh…what are you doing here?" I slowly put down the paint roller and swipe the sweat on my forehead with the back of my hand.

"I came to see if you wanted to go grocery shopping with me."

I frown, curious as to why she would want me to do something so menial with her. The confusion must be written all over my face, and I barely get out a single syllable before she interrupts me.

"I need to get the ingredients for Elisabeth's kringla. I offered to make it for Santa Day since…" She trails off, and her eyes get misty. Another person who can cry for Grandma when I can't. She recovers quickly. "I was hoping you'd know where her recipe card is so I don't mess it up."

"Yeah, I think so," I say as I awkwardly wipe my hands together. Aracely being sad affects me, sure, but it was the reminder of Santa Day that has me really shook up. It's Maple Park's pride and joy every Christmas season. A town celebration with a small parade that features Santa on the fire truck, the lighting of the memorial tree, a snowman building contest, more hot chocolate and baked goods than anyone could ever possibly eat, and of course, a chance for kids to sit on Santa's lap. The parade, snowman building, and memorial tree take place outside of the American Legion Hall, while the rest of the festivities are inside. For the much younger kids, there is a showing of a classic movie while they feast on snacks, then bingo and other games into the evening. For the adults, there's happy hour at BJ's and fireworks to close out the night.

I used to look forward to Santa Day every year. In fact, setting up for it was the first time Aracely and I kissed. The memory of the way she leaned into the kiss and gently pulled my hair sends a shiver down my back.

Grandma's kringla has always been a hit on Santa Day. She would spend an entire afternoon making dozens upon dozens of batches, separating them into baggies, and donating it all to the town so they could sell them for a profit on the day. Until this moment, I haven't even considered what it means that she won't be around to make it.

"So…" Aracely draws out the vowel. "Will you go with me? Please?"

I nod, oddly excited at the possibility of hanging out with her but also thrilled to do something so uniquely *Grandma.*

"Great," she says with relief. "I would have called or texted, but my number is still blocked."

I can feel my face and body get hot with embarrassment. "Oh, uh…" I scratch my neck nervously. "Sorry about that. I actually have a new number now. I'll give it to you."

She pulls her phone from her back pocket and hands it over. I quickly add myself as a contact and send a text message to my own phone so I can store hers as well.

"Okay," I say, and hand the phone back. "Let's go find that recipe card."

I easily locate Grandma's recipe in the box of index cards she kept inside the wooden hutch and snap a picture with Aracely's phone. We're at Wendell's Grocery within ten minutes, looking for the ingredients. I remember doing this with Grandma as a kid, and a newfound sense of giddiness fills me as I practically skip through the aisles looking for butter, vanilla, flour, and all the other odds and ends.

Wendell's is locally owned, so the prices are kind of steep, but the atmosphere is unmatched. There're garland and lights tucked into every single crevice. I take note of the mistletoe hanging above the back exit, and Aracely catches me looking.

"The purple ribbon is in BJ's."

"I know," I say quickly and don't miss the way her head tips questioningly at me. "I saw it when I had a few drinks with Pete the other day," I elaborate and anxiously clear my throat, slightly embarrassed she caught me looking.

We don't say much while shopping, just share a few stolen glances. It seems like everybody there is bustling around in preparation for the holiday, but we're just casually taking our time. This is something I've missed with Aracely. Everything has always been comfortable with her. Silences don't need to be filled, a simple look will tell me everything I need to know, and there's no rush to get away from each other and on to the next task.

As she reaches for a bag of flour, something dawns on me. "Do you still write about food?" She tilts her head but doesn't respond right away, so I continue. "Like you did in high school when you wrote up those food reviews on the school lunches."

She smiles at the memory. "You remember those?"

"Of course, they were always so funny. My favorite was how you described the way each lunch felt as it digested during basketball practice." A laugh bursts past my lips. Aracely had always enjoyed writing, too. Not as much as I did, but if it was about food, she could go on and on.

"Actually, I do write reviews for my students' stuff. They really enjoy it, especially when it's a bad review. I swear that sometimes, they leave out an ingredient on purpose just so I'll drag them and they can laugh about it later." She grabs some vanilla and places it in the cart.

I'm struck by how much extra time and effort she puts into her work at the school. Writing reviews for student chefs? That's above and beyond. "I'm surprised you even need a recipe card for kringla."

"Recipe cards are important. I can eye measurements and create things from scratch, but there are some classics you just don't mess with."

Once we make it to the checkout line, she turns to me. "So have you been writing while you're home?"

I curl my lips into my teeth. "Not really. Even before Grandma…" I let the unsaid hang between us. "I was having a slight case of writer's block. I can't seem to figure out an ending."

She starts to sort the items in our cart so it'll be faster when we reach the conveyor. "You'll figure it out, E. You created an entire universe and an elaborate story from nothing. I know you'll find a way to the ending, and it'll be perfect."

Her unwavering support actually makes me feel the slightest edge of confidence. Maybe I'll even open my computer tonight and attempt to write.

Maybe.

Probably not, but it's a nice thought.

My phone vibrates in my pocket. I reach for it and see Rae's name above the message: *Still waiting on that call. I HAVE BIG NEWS. Call me SOON.* I send a quick apology with a promise to call next time I'm free.

There's only one checker working and two very full carts in front of us. This is a part of small-town life I do not miss. I happen to like the convenience and quickness of self-checkouts and multiple lanes in the city. I sigh and tap my fingers on the cart.

"I like your books, by the way. I'm not sure if I've said that yet."

I straighten my shoulders with a bit of pride. "Thank you."

"I can see a lot of you in them."

It's not an insult, but I frown anyway. Grandma said something similar.

"What do you mean by that?" I ask with genuine curiosity. She hesitates, most likely worried about my reaction after the way I responded to her mentioning the correlation between Alma and my book earlier this week. "I ask because you're not the first person to say it," I offer as an explanation.

"Like…" She draws out the word. "The dry humor you have, the way the town resembles Maple Park, some of the names that I've already said." She chews on her bottom lip. "The grandmotherly oracle is very Elisabeth."

My chest tightens. "I see." I think I always knew these things, but it hits differently when its listed out like this. I guess I was more impacted by this place than I give it credit for.

"Oh." She snaps her fingers. "And the way you write about religion."

I laugh. That one was intentional. "Guess I'm not fooling anyone, huh?"

"And, um…maybe part of Joey and Sidney's relationship feels a little familiar?"

My head snaps in her direction. "What?"

"Nothing," she says quickly and waves her hand. "Never mind, it was stupid."

There's an awkward silence as I consider her suggestion. Have I really written a version of Aracely and me? Am I that transparent?

"So," she starts, and it's the nervousness in her voice that catches my attention. "Do you wanna maybe go get some coffee from Alma's before we head back?"

The tiniest bit of something blooms in my chest, and it makes my stomach flip in a satisfying way. "Yeah, that sounds good, actually."

We step up to the counter and finally start to check out. I'm more than a little excited at the prospect of catching up with Aracely and kicking myself for turning her down earlier in the week.

As we make our way through the tiny parking lot with our haul several minutes later, she spots some kids who appear to be selling something out of a box and gestures in their direction. I follow her wordlessly until I see they're selling puppies and stop dead in my tracks.

"No way," I say a little harshly. "If I take one step closer, I'm going home with a dog I don't need, nor did I ask for, and you'll be going home with an empty promise to me that you'll help out." I pull the open peacoat tighter to my body.

She barks out a laugh that reverberates off the few buildings in Maple Park's downtown. "Oh my God, Eli. That was one time, and

it was a hermit crab. Hardly something to hold over me forever."
She steps near me and links our arms.

I shift the groceries to my other hand and let her lead me toward
the box.

"Hi, Ms. Hernandez," one of the kids says excitedly. She can't
be more than fourteen, so I'm guessing she's a freshman.

"Hey, Tish," Aracely greets her as she looks in the box. "Selling
puppies?"

"Yeah, there's only one left. We started with six."

I peek into the box and see a tiny brown squirmy ball of what
appears to be some sort of bulldog mix.

"Aw." Aracely motions to the box. "May I?"

"Oh yeah, you can hold her," Tish says. "She's the runt of the
litter. She has her shots and is growing, though. She'd be the perfect
pet for you. Since they're not purebred, and we need them gone, I'll
give you a discount."

"You're quite the salesperson." Aracely turns to me and holds
the puppy out for me to take.

"No thanks," I say flatly. "Let's go get coffee instead."

"Oh, come on. She's so cute." She makes a show of holding her
up to my face.

"She looks like a potato."

Aracely pulls the puppy back to her chest and lightly scratches
under its chin. "I think you just named her. Potato." She puts her
nose right up against the puppy's and starts to baby talk. "Hi, Potato.
Do you wanna go home with Eli?"

"I hate you so much right now."

Her jaw drops, and she looks at me with such indignation I can
almost touch it. "Are you really going to not buy this *puppy* from
these *children* on *Christmas*?"

I make a show of rolling my eyes and turn to Tish. "How
much?"

Aracely fist pumps the cold air.

I groan. "You're a dick."

"I know," she practically sings. "We'll have to rain check that
coffee."

❖

Aracely and I walk back into the house laughing, even though I am still pissed she conned me with the puppy.

"Hey, where were you?" Tommy's voice comes from the kitchen as he steps out. "And what's that?" He motions to the wiggly worm in my arms.

"It's a potato," I say.

Aracely slaps my arm. "She got herself a little mental health gift from Wendell's parking lot. Her name is Potato."

"Why would you name a dog that?" says a voice that turns my veins to ice.

I freeze in place. My eyes go wide. I look at Tommy right as he mouths, "Sorry." Sorry for which part, though? Sorry he didn't warn me or sorry she's here at all?

When I don't answer, she steps out from behind Tommy. "Well?" she presses. "Why such a weird name?"

"Hi, Mom."

One week before Christmas, twenty-one years ago

I tuck my hair behind my ears for what feels like the billionth time. I'm definitely making it greasy with the oil from my hands.

"Why are you so nervous?" Aracely laces our fingers together to stop me from doing it again.

"You're meeting my mom," I repeat.

"Are you scared she won't be okay with us?"

"No." I shake my head. "That's not it."

Her frown lines deepen. "Why then?"

"She's not who she used to be." It's the understatement of the century, but I don't want to dive into all the gritty details with my girlfriend of almost a year. We've had so much fun getting to know each other, and I've shared almost everything with her. Almost. "She honestly was a really good mom when we were little and Dad was alive," I try to explain. "She changed after he died."

"Naturally," Aracely says as a way of explanation. "She lost the person she loves. Her companion. It makes sense she would change."

"Right," I continue. "But she made some bad choices, which I've kind of told you about."

"The drinking and pills."

I bury my face in my hands, embarrassed. "Yeah, that."

She pulls my hands down and cups my face. "She's human, Eli. She was hurting and made bad choices. She's trying to redeem herself. You can't punish her forever."

"I'm not," I say quickly and shake my head. "I don't. I'm just saying that the person she was before the drugs and the one after getting clean are very different." My throat tightens, and I swallow hard, trying to stop myself from crying. My mom is truly trying to do better again. She's had her highs and lows since getting arrested. Occasionally, I'll hear her voice in the stands at a basketball game, or I'll get a surprise phone call asking about my day. Those are few and far between. And her contact with us is very sporadic when she's dating someone new.

She shrugs. "I suppose that makes sense. People don't really stay the same after trauma."

"Yeah," I say. I look at my hands, thinking about all that was lost after Dad died.

She's quiet for a moment. "I'm sorry. I should just let you tell me. How is she different? What's making you nervous?"

I suck in a long breath through my nose and release it through my mouth. "She's a lot meaner. To everyone but mostly me. Like, I'm the only one who really gets under her skin."

"Why you?" she asks quickly and claps a hand over her mouth. "I interrupted, I'm sorry." The muffled apology comes through her fingers.

I lean forward to touch our foreheads. I drop a kiss on the tip of her nose and peel her hand from her mouth. I kiss her lips once, twice, three, four, and more times. I can never resist her lips. "It's okay," I say before one last kiss. "I don't know why. I think it's because I actually call her out when she's being cynical. Grandma says it's because we're too much alike."

"How was she before everything?" She tightens her grip on my hand.

"Loving. Affectionate. Doting. Focused."

"So a typical mom."

"Exactly. But now she's combative. She thinks I'm constantly out to hurt her. She always has an opinion as to why everything is stupid or wrong. I don't know." I shake my head and drop my eyes back to my hands in my lap.

"Did she go to therapy after your dad? After the addiction?"

I shrug. "I think so, for a little while. Not long enough. Not intensive enough."

"And she has no custody of you guys?"

I shake my head. "She gave it all to Grandma, but she's still around. She moves to wherever she has a new boyfriend. She lives in East Fork and works at Hy-Vee. It's the closest she's been to us."

"Is she…" She hesitates, but I know what she's asking.

"Clean?"

Her cheeks get rosy. She's embarrassed to have even asked.

"Kind of. She's done with the drugs, I know that. But she still drinks and claims that drinking was never her problem. I mean, I guess she's kind of right, but it would be nice if she just gave all of it up. She's a different person when she drinks." I feel bad for revealing all my mom's secrets to someone she's never met. My mother has been through hell, and I truly do feel for her. I just wish the old version of her would magically reappear. I want a mom who is there all the time. One who shows up constantly. One who stays positive. One who realizes the parent should care more. One who lets me be the kid.

"Different person than she used to be and different when she drinks," Aracely repeats. "Kinda sounds like she's two different people."

"There are definitely different versions of her. I hope you meet one of the better ones today."

"Well." She kisses my knuckles. "I look forward to meeting her, and no matter what she says, I recognize you are not one and the same. I love you regardless of whatever your mother may say to me."

I release a steadying breath. "She's going to love you. Everybody does."

She shrugs away my comment. "Maybe they do, but I only have eyes for you."

"Charmer."

"More like kiss-ass," she jokes and kisses my knuckles again.

Excerpt from The Stone River Series by Eli Thomas

Book One: The Curse

Abby looks so much like Joey's late sister it makes her blood freeze. Mary was a decent mother when Abby was a baby, but she fell away after her divorce was finalized. She was drinking too much and avoiding home too often.

When she got sick, Mary asked Joey to take custody of Abby. Through endless tears and soft sobs, Mary apologized to Abby and held her tight. She told her that her Aunt Joey would take good care of her and to always trust that Joey had her best interests in mind.

Joey and Abby were an odd pairing at first. They were both grieving, and neither of them knew how to exist together. Slowly, the twelve-year-old and the single, closeted woman in her thirties found a rhythm. It wasn't quite a mother-daughter bond, but there was mutual respect and understanding.

All of which makes the current situation more aggravating. Abby clearly knows something about what happened to Mason and may have even been with him that night. Joey recognizes that part of this may relate to typical teenage rebellion, but Abby is possibly endangering herself by staying quiet.

It drives Joey to her breaking point. "Listen, I'm not putting up with this silent bullshit anymore. You heard what Officer Cruz asked, now answer the question, or you're grounded."

"You can't ground me," Abby scoffs. "Nice try."

"I can, and I will. I already took the phone and TV out of your room this morning."

"You can't do that!"

"Then start talking." Joey chances a look at Sidney, who appears to be biting her lip and trying not to laugh.

"Fine," Abby says through gritted teeth.

Sidney clears her throat. "Abby, what happened in the cemetery that night?"

Abby shakes her head, still defiant.

Sidney pushes. "Was it something to do with Mason's church?"

"You mean his parents' cult?"

CHAPTER SIX: TAKE ME TO CHURCH

The night ended with Aracely making an awkward exit after my mom demanded everybody attend church together in the morning. Aracely goes to church every week with her mother, and Tommy also never misses because he went with Grandma. My mother's comments were directed at me and me alone. I didn't make much of a fuss over it at the time because I didn't think she'd even stick around, let alone follow through with an attempt to get me into one of my least favorite places.

I am up almost every hour throughout the night with Potato. What those little rat children failed to tell me is that she is not fully potty-trained. She pees all over my bed more than once, and when she does attempt to tell me with screams and yelps that she needs to go out, I barely make it down the steps and outside before she is leaking down the front of me.

Aracely and I went back into Wendell's and picked up some food for Potato after I bought her. I grimaced when she suggested I get a kennel or a crate for her. I know that seasoned pet owners train animals with the use of many different kinds of equipment. I am too weak for that. I have no experience, and I can't fathom putting this tiny, wiggly, whiney thing into any sort of enclosure. But at 3:30 in the morning, I wish I could kick my own ass as I lay down another layer of towels on the foot of my bed. The little worm cries unless she's sleeping curled against my face or on my chest.

I love the attention, but not at that ungodly hour.

So when my mother barges into my room just past seven

a.m. and announces that I have less than two hours to get myself presentable, my blood is already simmering, and my body is freezing from a lack of blankets.

I stumble down the stairs with Potato in my arms and the pee blankets slung over my shoulder. I carry her out the sliding back door and let her roam the fenced yard for a bit while I go and toss the blankets into the laundry room.

"I'm not going to church, Tommy," I say as I enter the kitchen where he's leaning casually against a counter.

He nods at me wordlessly and sips some milk from his cereal bowl. I can tell he went for a run this morning by the gel in his hair. He always showers and does his hair after his morning runs. I wasn't sure if he kept up with the running, but clearly, he has. I find myself a little jealous that I haven't continued my own exercise routine after playing sports. I've definitely gotten a little softer and bigger around my midsection.

"I mean it. I'm not going." I pull the robe I'm wearing tight around the loose pajamas and tie it shut.

He clangs his spoon into the bowl. "It would be easier to just give in. She's trying, Eli. This is how she tries." He's not wrong. Even after she and what's-his-name broke up years ago, she stayed in East Fork because it's somewhat close to us. Her random drop-ins became a bit of a routine. She managed, most years since I moved away, to stop by for at least an hour or so while I was in town. She found a new boyfriend. Then another. And another. None of them have stuck, but at least she has some consistency in her life without the moving around anymore. I suppose with the birth of her grandsons, these little visits will be happening more often. Especially since she retired last year from her job as a produce manager.

"She's not going to convince me by being a bully," I say, holding my nerve.

"Please just come with us. I can't handle one more thing right now. I'm too sleep deprived and stressed. I will literally start crying, and it'll be so awkward."

I grunt. "Please don't. I won't hug you." Neither of us enjoys being comforted by the other, even when we know we need it. He turns and puts his empty bowl in the sink.

Mom strides into the kitchen with a heavy sigh. "Eli, go get ready."

I clench my jaw. "I need to let Potato back in, and I'm not going to church."

"The dog is fine. He's a damn dog."

"She."

"What?"

"Potato is a she."

She waves her hand dismissively. "It doesn't matter. Go get dressed. We are going as a family."

"Since when do we do anything as a family?"

"Eli, please," Tommy begs from beside me. The look in his eyes tells me not to push this. Not right now. He was serious when he said he can't handle one more thing. His vulnerability gets to me. It's rare we ask things of each other.

I clench my jaw as a groan of frustration roars from my chest. "Fine," I practically spit as I walk back toward the stairs. "But I'm not saying a single prayer," I toss over my shoulder as I take the stairs two at a time.

❖

I was convinced that walking into my old church would only serve to annoy me, but everything from the smell to the decorations and the lighting all reminds me of Grandma. Sorrow builds, and any sense of annoyance has dissipated.

Until my mother starts talking.

She offers a good morning or a hello to every single person within arm's reach. They're feigning kindness, but the truth is, she hasn't gone to this church in so long that most probably don't even remember her. I would laugh in her face if I wasn't so mortified. The people who do remember her surely remember that she's gone batshit. The woman who lost her husband, her kids, and her damn mind. She drinks too much, talks too much, and acts like she's a born-again Christian when it's convenient.

I'm not exactly sure when my animosity toward my mother grew to such heights, but it was sometime after I graduated. She never called me after Aracely broke my heart, didn't bother to ask why I quit basketball, and rarely knows what's going on in my life. I was at my lowest low, and she wasn't there. It's not an easily forgivable thing. Instead of taking the high road, like Tommy did, I opted to wallow in self-pity, recognizing that I actually did lose both parents the day my dad died. For a few years, every time she even attempted to speak to me, she was met with an argument on my end. Never one to back down, she fought back, and our contentious relationship has yet to recover.

We make our way to the weekly greeters, and of course, it's Aracely and her mom. As we step up, I arch an eyebrow at Aracely, silently asking why she didn't mention yesterday that she would be greeting this morning.

She smiles in a way that says she's trying not to laugh. She pinches her lips together and doesn't even hide that she's clearly checking me out from head to toe. The way her eyes slowly creep up my body makes me wiggle in place. Out of disdain for every religious institution, I refused to get very dressed up, but I did manage to find a nice navy flannel to layer over a cream tank that cuts just a tad low for church. My red jeans are so tight, they're accentuating my legs and ass, but I hadn't even considered that when I got dressed. In fact, I hadn't thought much of my outfit at all until she makes a show of looking me over with such intensity. The hungry look in her eyes has effectively erased any and all of the self-consciousness I was feeling earlier about how I have gained weight and fell short on exercising the past few years.

"Aracely," I say.

"Eli," she whispers back. "Good morning." She extends her right hand, taking her greeting duties seriously. I take the opportunity to return the favor and drink her in. She's wearing a white blouse that has a few buttons undone at the top. Her hair is pulled back, revealing the length of her tan neck. Church or no church, I have an overwhelming desire to step forward and bite that perfect spot just below her ear. The way she used to moan when I would—

"Oh, good morning, Aracely." My mom cuts in front of me. She dodges Aracely's hand and goes straight for a hug.

I grimace and then groan when it's lasting too long. "Mom, that's enough."

Aracely smiles at me over her shoulder. "Good morning, Teri."

"How are you, dear?" She puts a hand on the side of Aracely's face. "Gosh, we miss not having you around as much."

"You've met her twice," I say under my breath but loud enough for both of them to hear. I glance at Aracely's mom, Jasmine. She's busy greeting another line of people who are eager to get into the main seating area of the church and get this show going. I'm envious of them and contemplate jumping lines.

"What are you up to these days?" Mom continues without acknowledging me.

I turn to Tommy. "Am I invisible? Is this a nightmare?"

He shrugs, obviously bored and ready to sit.

"I'm teaching at the high school for now. I've actually seen Eli quite a bit this past week since she's been subbing."

"That's nice to hear." She releases Aracely's face but keeps ahold of her hand. I don't think the sentence about me being a substitute teacher even registered in her brain. "And how about your love life? Married?"

"Jesus Christ, Mom," I practically shout.

That gets her attention, and her head snaps in my direction. "Elisabeth Thomas, you watch your mouth in the house of the Lord."

"Oh my God. Can we please just sit down and get this over with?"

Mom turns back to Aracely and apologizes for me. She finally releases her hand and walks toward the pews. Tommy grabs Aracely's hand, shakes it quickly with a low greeting of good morning, and follows Mom.

I mouth the words, "I'm sorry," as I shake her hand.

"Go say hi to my mom. She misses you."

I sidestep into the other line and wave at Jasmine. "Eli," she squeals and claps her hands. Her arms circle my neck, and she pulls me into a tight hug.

"Hi, Jasmine," I say into her shoulder. "How are you?" Aracely's mom hasn't changed since I met her. I would swear she's not even aging at a normal human rate if it wasn't for the few gray hairs adorning her head. She's short, spunky, and the most genuinely loving person I've ever met. Aracely never knew her father, and according to her, she didn't need to because her mom filled two parental roles better than most people fill one.

I would definitely agree.

"Oh, I'm fine. I sure do miss seeing you." She releases me and motions to the main doors. "I better not keep you. Please stop by the house before you leave town. I'd like to catch up over dinner or something. And I'm so sorry about your grandmother. Elisabeth was really special."

"She was." I squeeze her shoulders one last time, appreciating her willingness to move the greeting line along, unlike other mothers I know.

We're not even through the opening hymn, and I'm yawning. My mom pinches my side, and I jump. "What was that for?" I yell-whisper over the melody of voices.

She shushes me. "Stop yawning, it's rude."

"I'm tired. I was up all night with Potato."

I turn to Tommy on the other side of me, but he's choosing to ignore our entire exchange and sing along with the rest of the congregation. He looks far more tired than me. As a new parent, he's definitely exhausted. His hair is disheveled despite the gel, his shirt is buttoned wrong, and I can tell his facial hair is getting longer than he's comfortable with. I catch a weakening in myself when I realize how much he looks like Dad.

"And," I add, turning back to Mom and forcing down my feelings, "you don't even belong to this church anymore. Why is it so important that you're seen here?" I look her over. She definitely puts on a good show. Her hair and makeup are done, her clothes are clean, well-fitting, and colorful.

"It's not, Eli. I'm here for my kids. They lost their grandmother, and I'm trying to offer some support. Why are you being like this?"

"Why don't you ask me what I need instead of forcing what you think I need?" I rub my tired eyes. I'm so sick of having the same fight with my mom over and over again. She hasn't even legally been my parent in over thirty years. "Why didn't you just come to Grandma's funeral if that's how you feel?"

She doesn't respond right away, so I turn and look at her. She's facing forward, refusing to meet my eyes. Tears build and slowly spill down her cheeks. "I haven't been to a funeral since your dad di—" She chokes on the last word. I reach out to touch her shoulder and comfort her, but she waves me off. "I'm fine. It's just that his funeral was in this same church. It's hard enough to come here for a service, let alone a funeral."

I sigh and let go of the tension in my shoulders, relaxing them and my body into the pew. For all her faults and all of the times she was an absent mother, I still feel inclined to comfort her. "Okay," I whisper. "I understand that, but I'm not even religious, Mom. I don't believe in God. I don't go to church. This"—I circle my finger to indicate everything around me—"is stupid to me."

She turns to me, more tears following the ones that just dripped off her chin, and I regret my word choice. I don't appreciate her antics, but it's never my intention to hurt her. "Why do you always have to make everyone around you feel so small?"

The singing has stopped, and the reverend has taken his place at the front. As he begins to do his hand motions and repeat a prayer, everyone diligently bows their heads.

Instead of apologizing, I set my jaw and double down. "You should have just come to her funeral."

"Both of you," Tommy leans across my lap, "Shut up. For the love of everything. Shut. Up."

The reverend finishes his opening blessing just as I'm about to rip into Tommy, and a loud chorus of "Amen" stops me.

"Please rise," is the instruction from the front.

I sigh, defeated, and stand.

❖

The rest of the day is shockingly even more trying than the forced church service. Mom follows Tommy and me home, helps us make lunch while criticizing the entire thing, falls asleep on the couch while scrolling on her phone, and then wakes up and asks Tommy to start drinking with her since it is "reasonably enough" past noon.

"I'm good, Mom," Tommy declines as nicely as possible. He goes back to drying the dishes and carefully putting them away. My heart constricts at the sight. Grandma taught us proper housekeeping skills. Washing, drying, and putting away the dishes is a routine after every meal. I was helping him only a moment before and have retired to the table to write thank-you notes to people who sent us money, flowers, and gifts for the funeral. I also still need to send the papers from Lara's office back to her. We begrudgingly signed what we needed to and decided to figure it out on our own without bothering Lara or her office any further.

Mom scoffs. "Fine." She rolls her eyes. "Just get me a beer from the fridge." I guess the church version of Mom has left, and the drinking personality has entered the game.

He dries his hands and doesn't bother to turn, probably scared of her reaction. "We don't have any alcohol in the house, Mom."

"Why not?" When neither of us answers, she grunts again. "Fine, well, one of you is gonna have to take me to get some from Wendell's."

"Do you really need it?" I press, knowing I'm entering dangerous territory.

"Eli," Tommy whispers, chastising me.

Mom barely acknowledges it. She shrugs and sits across from me. "I'm on vacation. I deserve to relax."

I frown and push a card inside an envelope, then reach for another. "Vacation? This is a vacation?"

She grabs some holiday-themed chocolates from Grandma's candy dish to the side of us. She pops them in her mouth and chews loudly. "Yeah, vacation. I'm away from my home and visiting my family. I'm relaxing."

"I'll go to the store, Mom." Tommy tries to beat me to the punch. He quickly strides to the coat closet, slides on an extra layer, and reaches for his shoes near the door.

"You're less than an hour from home and visiting family because your former mother-in-law has died. Hardly a vacation. Just say you want to drink because you want to drink."

"God, everything has to be such a production with you. Fine, I want to drink. Happy?"

"Not even a little. I hate when you drink. It changes you. May as well be popping pills again."

"Eli," Tommy shouts.

Mom slams her hand on the table so hard, I'm scared it may actually buckle under the force. "You stop it right now!" She's already crying. She always does this. Instant tears and guilt whenever we fight back. It's never her fault. "You think you know everything, and you don't."

I roll my eyes. "Believe it or not, it's not my goal in life to be mean to you. Can you, for once, just consider I'm asking about your drinking because it's a problem?"

"How would you even know? You never see me. You never call. You never visit. You're so selfish." She sets her mouth and folds her arms to show that *now*, she's really mad.

"You never raised me. Why should I want to do those things? And I'm selfish? You chose narcotics and alcohol over us more than once. I'm allowed to ask questions." My voice is rising. I know I'm losing control, and I'm about to say something I'll regret.

"I can't with you, Eli. I can't even believe we have the same genes. You think everybody in church this morning is so ignorant—"

"Because they are."

"And that I'm so stupid—"

"Well, when you act like this."

"But you don't know everything, Eli."

"Then please, prove me wrong."

"You hurt people."

"Because I'm honest? How does—"

"You hurt your grandmother."

That one stops me. She notices, and because she's not accustomed to me giving in, she hesitates for just a second before twisting the knife.

"It's true." She swipes at her tears and rubs her nose. "She said it more than once. You abandoned her and Tommy here. It was more than just moving away. You ran away, and you didn't even get to say good-bye to her. I might be a bad mom, but you're not a much better granddaughter."

My mouth opens, but only silence fills the air. We're suspended in time as the gravity of what my mother has accused me of settles over the room like a weighted blanket that slowly suffocates me.

I close my mouth.

Tommy, appearing from somewhere behind me, slams his fists on the table, effectively sending the vase of flowers and all the thank-you cards flying to the ground. Shockingly, the vase doesn't shatter, but the action has the intended impact. Both my mother and I turn to him, wide-eyed.

"Fuck you both," he seethes. "Neither of you has room to talk about her. To cry over her. You weren't here. This is supposed to be the happiest week of my life. My babies were born, but instead, I'm dealing with a dead grandma, a faulty will, and the two of you." He straightens his shoulders and walks to the door.

"Where are you going?" Mom asks with a hint of aggression. "Are you going to Wendell's? I'll go with you."

"No," he scoffs back at her. "I might sugarcoat things more than Eli, but she's right, Mom. You're a drunk, and you need help. I'm not getting you alcohol. I'm going to see my kids, and I thought, just maybe, you wouldn't make this about you and would want to see your grandsons."

"I'll come with," she repeats desperately.

"You're not invited," he snaps. He walks to the door, and with his hand on the doorknob, he looks at me. "And you. You can't just…never mind. Not worth it."

Tommy slams the door behind him so hard that both Mom and I jolt.

I leave wordlessly right after. Mom doesn't try to stop me. I can hear her muffled sobs. I'm sure later on, we'll both hear about how awful we treat her, but for the time being, I need away from her and away from the house.

I drive to Pete's, but when I turn onto his street, I can see his kids outside playing in the yard. He's in his garage, clearly looking for something and attempting to spend time with them. I can't bring myself to interrupt his Sunday afternoon with his family, so I just keep driving.

I drive and drive and drive some more. I cover every street of Maple Park at least six times at a snail's pace. I'm trying and failing to cry. I need to cry. I need to grieve for my grandmother. I need to cry over not knowing what she was trying to tell us with the will. I want to cry for Tommy and for how sorry I am. I even need to cry over my mom and how we've never had a true relationship.

Hours pass, my car is getting low on gas, and the sun is sinking. It gets dark well before six p.m. this time of year, and before I realize it, the holiday lights are glowing, and I'm parked outside the city park, admiring how beautiful all the maples and evergreens look lit up. Even as an adult, I'm mesmerized.

I open my phone for the first time since I left the house and see a missed call from Mom and a voice mail that I definitely won't be listening to right now. Or maybe ever.

I write a text to Tommy, spouting off a quick apology. If there's one thing he and I have always been good for, it's forgiving one another.

The gas light comes on as I let the car idle. I'm just about to resign and head to Pump It when a loud rap on my driver's side window makes me yelp and grab my chest. I turn and see Aracely, all bundled up and cute, smiling at me through the frosted window. I roll the window down. "What are you doing?"

She leans into the car, probably to feel some of the warmth. With the window down, I can tell the temperature has dropped nearly twenty degrees since the sun set. "Hi," she says with an impossibly big smile. "I saw you driving around town about ten different times this afternoon, so when you finally parked, I thought I'd make us some hot chocolate, and we could go for a walk through the park?"

I feel my cheeks get warm, embarrassed she spotted me. "How did you know I parked?"

She points past my face to a house on the edge of the street that lines the park trails. "My mom lives there now."

"You mean, you both live there now."

She playfully nudges my shoulder with her fist. "Yes, fine. I live there now. So what do you say? Stroll through the park? You clearly have something on your mind."

In this moment, I'm actually thrilled she knows me so well. "Where's this hot chocolate you speak of?"

She proudly holds up a thermos. "We're gonna have to share." She reaches into her pocket with her free hand and produces some extra gloves and a stocking cap with a poof ball. "I also brought these, just in case you didn't have any with you."

"I don't. This coat is barely warm enough, so thank you."

"Is that a yes?"

"It's a yes."

She bounces in place with excitement before stepping back and gesturing for me to get out. "Milady."

"You're still such a dork." I roll up the window, turn off the car, and step out into the cold, tightening my coat around me. I shiver. "Brr."

"You used to find my dorkiness endearing." She hands me the gloves and hat. I eagerly cover myself.

"I still do," I assure her. As I pull on the final glove, my body stills at the feeling of Aracely's nimble fingers toying with the buttons on the peacoat. She has removed her own gloves to button it up for me. The tenderness of the moment has my heart brimming with something I haven't felt in a long time: cared for.

Slowly, she smooths the collar, tucks my loose hair under my chin, and pats my shoulders. "There." She slides her gloves back on and reaches for the thermos she deposited on the roof of my car.

My silence must unnerve her a bit because she turns to me with wide eyes. "What?"

"Nothing, just cold."

"Yeah, sorry, I didn't bring an extra scarf. Do you want mine? Here." She pulls the scarf off her own neck so fast, I don't even have time to argue with her. She hands me the thermos and quickly wraps the flannel around my neck. She tucks it into the front of the borrowed coat and reaches around to softly remove my long hair from under the scarf and lay it gently on top. "I know I've already mentioned it, but your grandma loved this coat."

"I can imagine she did," I whisper. "It's not really my style."

"It's not, but you still wear it well."

Her face is so close that it would take virtually no effort to turn and lightly kiss her. I can smell her hair, her perfume, and something that has always been distinctly her. It's a scent I wish I could live inside for the rest of my days. Without even thinking, I let my eyes drift close and slowly inhale.

Aracely.

Back when we were dating, I used to joke that I wanted to climb inside her closet and live there forever because it smelled like her.

When I open my eyes, she's pulled back and staring at me. She's not judging me in the slightest. If anything, she realizes what I'm doing and is welcoming it.

"Shall we?" She motions in the direction of the paved trail that leads through the illuminated park.

"We shall," I confirm. "May I open this hot chocolate?"

"I'd be offended if you didn't."

We slowly make our way down the trail and into the frosty lights. I carefully unscrew the lid to the thermos and pause to pour a little bit of the drink into the lid. Instantly, the hot liquid against the cold air creates a billow of steam that warms my face as I blow on it.

It will never be sufficiently cool enough to not burn my mouth, so I just go for it and sip. I lose the entire top layer of my tongue, but I can't bring myself to care because it's so warm, and I can feel its effect before I even swallow. The chocolate is thick enough to taste through the burn. I hum with appreciation and slowly start walking again. "This is good."

"You should have let it cool off longer."

"There's no time for that."

She laughs and reaches for the lid as we keep our steady pace. She chances a small drink, and her face hilariously contorts into a look of pain and shock. She barely manages to swallow before coughing. "Eli, that is scalding. Let it cool off."

"No way, I've already filled my mouth with blisters, there's no going back now." I take another sip and make a satisfied noise.

We walk in silence for a bit. At first, I get lost in looking at all of the lights and the clear night sky while cradling the hot chocolate. Then, before I even realize I'm doing it, I get lost watching Aracely. Her eyes reflect the colors of the lights, and her face is rosy with the biting cold. She's just as beautiful as ever. The aging process has been good to her, and it makes me realize that I don't know much about her life since she broke up with me. I know she's had at least one other relationship. I witnessed it firsthand years ago. I know what she's told me since I've been home, but that's about it. Did she travel? Did she enjoy college? Did she double major in culinary arts and nutrition like she had originally planned? Where else has she lived? For the first time ever, I'm genuinely sad I don't know much about her life from the past two decades.

She turns and bashfully drops her eyes. "So what's on your mind? Why were you out doing one of your angry drives?"

I sip the last of the hot chocolate from the lid and screw it back on the thermos before placing it in my pocket. "I forgot you know that about me. No point in denying it, I guess." I shrug and take a deep breath. "I got into a fight with my mom."

Aracely, to her credit, just nods along. I'm sure she has plenty of opinions on the matter, considering she knows quite a bit of my past.

"She's so infuriating. And what pisses me off more is I upset Tommy because of it."

She links her arm through mine and pulls me closer. I'm not sure if it's to comfort me or for body heat. "Thomas Thomas will be fine. He's just had a really long and emotional week. He's a very forgiving person."

I snort a laugh at her use of Tommy's given name. Even though I'm the one who tortured him over it while growing up, I still occasionally forget his legal name is actually Thomas Thomas. I'm not sure I've ever heard the whole story as to why, but the one we've been told most often is that Dad messed up writing down his name for the birth certificate. He was supposed to be Devin Thomas, but somehow ended up Thomas Devin Thomas. They never bothered to use his middle name, nor did they attempt to get it fixed. At the time, my parents were young and in love, and my mother was sober. He became Tommy, and I don't think anybody could imagine him any other way.

Silence falls back over us until we come to a small clearing lined with glowing candy canes and a lighted gazebo. To the left of the gazebo is the largest evergreen tree in the park, the brightest one by far. Someone managed to get speakers and music hooked up so the lights dance with the music. I glance around as Aracely stares at the tree. I find it odd there's nobody out walking and looking at this right now.

"Where is everybody? Why are we the only ones here?" I ask seriously.

"Maybe it's too cold." She shrugs. "And it's a school night."

It makes enough sense that I don't push it.

"I did hear some sirens earlier. I hope it was nothing bad, but that might also be a reason," she continues.

I didn't hear anything, but it might have been when I was driving on the other side of town with my music up. I glance at the sky just as big fluffy snowflakes start to fall all around us. I haven't been keeping track of the weather, so I wasn't expecting the snow. I stare at the tree and soak in the beauty of it as the snow gently falls.

"Thank you," I say quietly. "For this. You didn't have to come out in the cold and bundle me up and feed me hot cocoa to cheer me up."

"Of course I did. I will always want to take care of you, you know that."

I turn and face her. "I've been awful to you. Not just lately either. For a long time."

"It's okay—"

"It's really not," I interrupt. I know she'll attempt to take some of the blame and say it's in the past and whatever other excuse she's about to let me use. My mom's accusations, however misguided or fueled by her own issues, weren't completely untrue. I haven't been good. Aracely never deserved the cold way I treated her after she dumped me. She was completely allowed to make that decision for her own future. And she wasn't wrong about it all. I did find success I wouldn't have found staying here. "If it's okay with you, I'd like to catch up sometime and get to know the adult version of you." She remains silent. "I'm sorry, Aracely, I never should—"

I'm cut off by the force of her lips covering mine and my heart dropping to my stomach. Her lips are warm and cover my bottom lip like they were meant to fit there forever. I pull back just enough to breathe and push forward again. This time, I take her bottom lip and drag my tongue lightly across it. Kissing Aracely is like a first relaxing dip in a hot bath, and my entire body feels it. I'm lighter. I'm happier. I'm eager for more.

I wrap my arms around her and grip her coat while pulling her impossibly closer. Her hands slide up my cold face and tangle in my hair. She gently pulls in a way that makes a small moan escape my throat. I haven't forgotten how to kiss her, and apparently, she hasn't forgotten how to make me tick, either.

I smile against her lips and tilt my head to deepen the kiss, finally recognizing the feeling from when Aracely asked me for coffee at Wendell's.

Hope.

Christmas Eve, twenty years ago

I'm so bored sitting through the Christmas Eve midnight service—actually held at eight p.m.—I could cry. I'm chomping my gum and letting my head loll back and forth so much that I'm getting a little dizzy. I catch Aracely's gaze from across the aisle and one row ahead of me and smile at her. She motions for me to pay attention and then winks.

She and I had a conversation the night before in between heated kisses about how I would rather be cleaning up literal shit off the streets than sitting through this church service. Aracely has never made me feel bad for not believing in anything the church force-feeds me, so I do my best not to make her feel attacked for her beliefs. But sometimes, I can't just sit and take it. I used to be indifferent about religion. I never bought into the baby savior story that Christianity spins, and even when I was very young, I never understood why people considered *their* religion to be the *right* one. Especially when there are so many of them. My indifference grew to resentment when I was fourteen and a pastor told me that gay people should be excommunicated and animals don't go to heaven. I'm sure I could have appeased such a horrible experience by simply talking to my grandma about it, but instead, I decided religion is stupid.

Grandma reaches over and pinches my leg after I direct an air kiss in Aracely's direction.

"Ow," I whisper. "What? I'm not doing anything wrong."

"Don't start with me, young lady," she whispers back. "You

promised you'd behave for this one. Don't make me wish I'd left you at home."

"*I* wish you had. This is boring and pointless."

Tommy leans forward and looks past Grandma at me. "Shush!"

"Oh, blow me, Tommy." I cross my arms.

Grandma takes a moment before she turns to me again. "I will always respect your wishes, Eli. I know you don't buy into religion, and you find it difficult to blindly trust such an oppressive institution." She's using my own words against me. This was my exact argument last week as to why I didn't want to go. "But I asked you to join me for the Christmas service because it is important to me. I want you here because I love you. I want to share the important things in my life with the ones I love. I'm not asking you to pray, but please just respect the place where I feel safe."

"Jesus." I roll my eyes. "Way to lay it on thick, Grams."

"Where do you think you get it?" She nudges me with her shoulder, and I smile despite myself.

I look around a few more times, refusing to listen to a sermon about wise men, before I turn back to Grandma. "Can I open a present tonight?"

Her look is pointed. "Don't start that."

"I actually agree with Eli on this," Tommy interjects.

Grandma shakes her head. "You two. Kids at heart when it comes to Christmas."

"Is that a yes?" I ask.

"Fine, but you have to be quiet for the rest of the service."

I mime zipping my lips shut. I look back at Aracely, who is muffling a laugh, knowing I just got scolded.

"Do you want to invite Aracely and her mom over tonight?"

I frown, doubting the offer. "Really? It'll be almost nine o'clock."

She lowers her head to whisper while the congregation watches the little kids file to the front and perform their Christmas concert. "It'd be nice to have them over for some hot chocolate and a movie. We could even build the fort." It's a Christmas tradition.

I nod frantically. "Yeah, I'll text her now."

I reach for my phone, but Grandma stops my hand. "No, don't text in church, it's tacky."

"Okay, I'll wait until after." I turn my attention back to the little kids singing about being away in a manger for approximately twenty seconds before I'm bored again. "Santa Day was fun yesterday," I whisper.

"Is it literally impossible for you to be quiet at church?" she whispers back.

"Yes." I tap my knees. "I heard your kringla was the star of the show."

"Always is."

That earns her a smile from me. "Last year at Santa Day is when Aracely and I first started talking." Yesterday, we went and kissed under the same mistletoe with the purple ribbon. We were both shivering after the parade but forced ourselves to go and complete the act inside Wendell's, eight blocks from the Legion where the rest of the festivities take place.

She hums. "I know, honey. You haven't shut up about her in one year and one day."

Despite our basketball season being off to a rocky start, I'm the happiest I've ever been this time of year. "I'm in love with her." The confession takes me by surprise. I'm so shocked, my eyes bulge. "I told her two days ago." I can't stop confessing. It must be the church effect.

She taps my bouncing leg. "Relax, dear. Falling in love is a wonderful experience. No need to be so nervous."

"I'm just scared if I make it too real, I'll lose it." I look at Aracely again, and my chest tightens. She's watching the little kids sing and whispering with her mom. I don't want to lose her like I lost my parents.

"Don't be scared to speak your truth, Eli. Life is too short to hide our feelings." She turns to the front and stretches her neck. She bounces in place slightly when the music changes over. "'Go Tell It on the Mountain.' This one is my favorite. It reminds me of your dad."

That was something I didn't know. "Why?"

"When he was little and did these concerts, he was such a passionate singer that we could hear him belting out that song above everyone else. People laughed and were entertained, but he didn't care. He just kept on singing, loud and proud."

Tears fill my eyes, which is rare when talking about my father. I've been so far removed from him and from the life we had with him. It's different for Grandma, though. He was her baby. She created him, nurtured him, raised him. She loved him more than she loved anything else in this life, and she had to bury him, too. His death changed my mom, but it broke my grandmother. I can see it in her eyes. She stayed strong for us because she had to, but I can't even imagine her pain. "I like that story."

She looks at me, tears in her eyes, too, and says, "Me too, honey. Me too."

CHAPTER SEVEN: BIG FEELINGS

When Aracely and I finally parted last night, she quietly walked me back to my car while we stared at the lights above and all around us. My mind was reeling with what had just happened, but the rest of me was surprisingly calm. The silence was comfortable, and her body language was nothing but loving.

Once we reached the car, she placed the softest kiss I've ever had on my forehead and then another on my lips. She whispered good night and carefully tucked me inside my car. I drove in a daze back to a dark house. I let Potato out to pee and cleaned up all the spots where she had accidents since my mother and brother had clearly both left for the night. I'm assuming Mom returned to East Fork since it's not too long a drive, and Tommy is probably still with one of his children.

As I settle into bed with the little furball curled up next to me, I set my alarm to go to the school in the morning. Pete texted that he needed someone to cover in the science department. While on my phone, I delete my mom's voice mail without even listening to it. I can already predict what she wants to say to me. This one will be filled with utter disdain for how I spoke to her and what I did. It'll be followed by an apology text or voice mail tomorrow asking for forgiveness and a promise to do better. If there is one thing my mom has always been good for, it's a follow-up apology. Something I am not so skilled in.

I set my phone on the nightstand and briefly contemplate lifting the facedown photo. Aracely has an identical copy. I wonder if she still has it, and I wonder once again if she was actually successful in falling out of love with me. Over the years, I dwelled on if she ever cried over me, missed me, thought about me, etc., and I assumed she lost all love for me like she said she would.

My body, still completely at ease, is relaxing more and more by the second. Even my crippling writer's block can't reach me right now. My mind is jumping so quickly from one topic to the next that it feels like I'm suspended in a hypnotic state. I close my eyes, and before I drift off, my last thought is that I didn't realize how much I was *still* missing Aracely Hernandez until she kissed me under those Christmas lights.

❖

When I show up to school the next morning, the euphoria of the night before drains out of me in a brutal way. The sirens Aracely heard were from a car accident. A bad one. A student was involved, and she was really hurt.

Pete catches me by the arm as I'm about to head to the science room. "Eli, hang on." His eyes are bloodshot, and his throat is scratchy.

"Pete," I say with sympathy, "I'm so sorry. Is she going to make it?"

"Yeah, she's just really hurt. Her brain. Her spine." He chokes on the words. I step forward to comfort him, but he waves me off. "I'm okay for now. I need you to check on Aracely. I can't find her, and she's close with Dana."

"Is Dana…" I hadn't heard the student's name until now.

He nods. "She's not in her classroom, but I know she's here somewhere. I have counselors meeting with students and Dana's friends, but nobody is checking on my staff. Would you be willing? Since you know her more personally?"

I nod. "Not a problem."

Old intuition sends me looking for Aracely in the girls' locker room near the gym. We have both had our fair share of secret cries in there. As soon as I enter, I know she's hiding in one of the private showers. She can't see me, but I can hear her. The sound of her cry, heartbreakingly, is unmistakable to me.

"Cely?" I say quietly so as to not startle her.

She stifles a sniffle. "Yeah?"

"Pete wanted me to check on you. I thought I might find you here."

She laughs through a sob. "Of course you did."

I get into the stall next to hers and close the curtain. We're separated by a six-foot brick wall but can still hear one another. "I locked the door," I tell her. "So feel free to talk openly."

"Thank you," she barely whispers. "I just need a minute before I have to comfort others."

"You're close with her? Dana?"

"Yeah." She hiccups another sob. "I dodged her on Friday. I was so tired and wanted to go home. I knew she was coming in to ask for help with something, but I told her it could wait until Monday." I hear her breath stagger as she sucks in a deep breath. "I shouldn't have done that. She's just a kid."

"You couldn't have known. You're allowed to be human." Hearing Aracely struggle is actually bringing me closer to tears than I have been since Grandma's funeral. I want to comfort her. I want to crawl around this wall and envelop her in my arms, but I know better. Aracely wants space, or she wouldn't be hiding. She'll tell me when she's ready for me to come to her.

She doesn't say anything, but I can hear her breathing start to even out.

I test the waters. "You okay?"

"Yeah," she says with a far steadier voice than before. "How'd you lock the door?"

"Pete gave me a master key so I could get into any room to sub."

She snorts. "Of all the people he could give a master key to, he chooses a temporary sub."

"Yeah." I huff a laugh at the irony of it and jangle the key and badge that are on a lanyard around my neck. "Too bad I didn't have this when we used to sneak in here."

That earns me a genuine laugh that echoes off the walls. "Lock or no lock, it didn't stop us from hooking up in these showers almost every week."

"Nothing, and I can't stress this enough, *nothing* could get me to keep my hands off you back then."

She makes a satisfied noise with a teasing tone. "Too bad it's not still that way now that we have a key."

I smile and feel my cheeks get red. I'm actually glad she can't see me right now.

"Sorry," she says when I don't reply. "Did I cross a line?"

"No," I say quickly. "No, not at all. You just made me bashful is all."

I hear her shuffling around and a curtain being pulled back, quickly followed by the curtain in front of me. I scramble to my feet and get my balance just as she surges forward and kisses me with such force, I nearly fall right back over.

I tangle one hand into her long hair while gripping her back with the other. She wastes no time slipping her tongue into my mouth and pushing me against the shower wall. I'm jammed between the knobs and the corner of the stall, but I can't find it in me to care about where I am or the cleanliness of the area. I bite her bottom lip the way I know she likes, and it makes her pause with a slight moan. She retaliates by nudging my head and attaching her lips to the side of my throat. It's a sensitive spot and sends my hips bucking into her, looking for more friction. I don't think this is what Pete had in mind when he asked me to come find her.

I barely register what her hand is doing between us before her nimble fingers have managed to undo my belt. A surge of excitement pulses through me and coils in my stomach. She's just about to dip her hand inside my pants when I break the kiss.

"Wait," I say, dizzy from arousal. "Just hang on." I take a steadying breath, trying to regain focus. "I came in here to comfort you. We don't have to do this."

"I know we don't have to. I want to."

"You're projecting. Hiding. I don't know, something a therapist would say about how you're trying to not feel grief, so you're using sex as an outlet."

She steps back but keeps her hands firmly and confidently on my body. "Eli, that might be partially true in the moment, but I can assure you that I want you. I have wanted to get you naked *literally* every second since I saw you two weeks ago."

"Oh." My voice squeaks. I was unprepared for that answer, and I have no answer for what it is currently doing to my body. "Okay," I affirm as I grab the waistline of her pants and pull her back into me. I go for her lips, but she evades me and lands right back on my neck. "Oh shit," I gasp and then moan.

She smiles against my neck. "There's my girl. Never quiet."

The comment snaps me out of whatever turned-on stupor she's put me in, and I push her away. Probably too roughly. "I'm sorry," I say quickly.

She frowns, obviously confused, and I can't blame her. "What's wrong?"

"I just…I don't know. You called me your girl, and it made me realize where I am and what I'm doing, and…" I suck in a deep breath and rub my face.

"And what?"

"And I'm not this person anymore," I say, exasperated. I throw my hands up and let them fall at my sides. I know it's childish, but everything about being back home has made me feel like I'm actually regressing. The past has a way of wrapping itself around me and pulling me back. I may need some closure, but I know I don't want to be the same girl who got her heart broken, who lost her parents, and then ran away. "I've moved on. I've outgrown this town, and I don't want to repeat it."

I meet her eyes, expecting to see hurt, offense, maybe anger, but I get none of those. "You're right."

"I am?" I frown, not expecting that response and feeling stupid for arguing with her about my own point.

"Yes, you did outgrow this town. You outgrew your past. You outgrew our teenage relationship. But guess what?" She steps forward and refastens my belt.

"What?" I whisper, genuinely scared of what she's about to say.

She leans in and whispers back. "I grew up, too." She places a kiss on my forehead. "We change and grow, Eli, that's part of life. Just because you're bigger than who you were as a teenager doesn't mean you can't find happiness in some of the old places you used to. Some of the old people."

"Aracely, I didn't mean—"

"You didn't offend me, so don't even start with that. I'm just saying it doesn't matter that you've evolved. I'd be disappointed if you hadn't. Life changes all of us…" She pushes some stray hairs behind my ear. "But it doesn't change what's in my heart."

I tilt my head at the last comment. "Your—"

"I love you, Eli. I'm in love with you. I've never stopped loving you for even one second since we were sixteen years old."

"Cely, you—"

"Broke up with you. I know. I did it for what I thought was your own good. And I know what I said. And I know I chose money over love." She swallows hard and takes a step back. "But hey, I was a kid. And at least I was right about part of it because you are, after all, a wealthy and successful writer."

"But—"

"I'm not going to stop loving you, ever." She says it with such finality that I finally stop trying to interject. "Elisabeth Thomas, I will always love you. Do whatever it is you need to do in this life to find yourself and come to terms with it. If you never love me back again, then so be it. I'll die knowing I loved you without terms attached. If you leave town again and decide you don't want me, fine. I'll move on as much as I can." She takes another step back and waits until I look her in the eyes. "You probably thought I was going to give some kind of ultimatum, but it would be bullshit because the truth is, you could leave tomorrow, and I could move on enough to settle down and marry someone else. But if you came back and said you were ready to be with me, that other person would be null and void. You are it for me. You were my first love, you'll be my last love, and my only love. I can find happiness elsewhere. I just don't *want* to. I want you and only you."

"Aracely," I start and stop. My mouth opens and closes a few times. "I don't know what to say." After all this time, she decides she was wrong? That we can't fall out of love and move on? I spent so long agonizing over her words. I spent so many years trying to convince myself she didn't love me. I'm finally getting the answers to my questions and hearing exactly what I thought I wanted to hear for so long. So why doesn't this feel like closure? "This is a lot."

She strokes the side of my face from a distance. "You don't have to say anything. Just don't get in your own way. Do what makes you happy, Eli. That's truly all I've ever wanted."

There's a loud banging at the door, signaling the end of our time together. I can hear some muffled voices through the door.

"Guess we'll have to finish this conversation another time," she says sadly. She swipes under her eyes, trying to fix her makeup after crying, and leaves me with a quick wave.

Three days before Christmas, twenty years ago

Aracely bounds through my bedroom door and tackles me backward onto my bed. Through quick, forceful kisses, she manages to say, "Hi."

After another barrage of quick kisses all over my face, I say, "Hi," back to her.

She sighs and plants a final kiss on the tip of my nose. "I missed you."

"You were here this morning."

"I know. It doesn't matter. I miss you all the time."

I run my fingers through her long hair and kiss her forehead. "I missed you, too."

She adjusts her body and starts to buck her hips into mine.

My eyes bulge. "Cely!" I push her shoulders back and attempt to sit up. "My grandma and brother are downstairs."

"Didn't stop you last night." She waggles her eyebrows.

"They were sleeping. Tommy leaves his TV on all night, and Grandma has that breathing machine. There's no way they heard us." But even as I say it, I start to question if it's true. The walls are thin.

"Not me. You, on the other hand…" She clicks her tongue.

I feign offense. "How dare you? I was a perfectly proper lady. I had a silent orgasm."

She snorts and kisses the corner of my mouth. "Forgive me, my perfectly proper lady, but you left bite marks on my shoulder." She pulls my hand to her lips and kisses my knuckles.

I pull my hand back. "Oh my God, seriously? I did?" I pull at the collar of last year's state basketball T-shirt that she's wearing. She always says it's her favorite shirt because she has my name on her at all times. The shirt has the names of the entire basketball roster, but details aren't important. I can see the tiniest hint of a bruise on her shoulder. "Oh, that's not so bad. Want me to darken it?" I say and tickle her neck.

She wiggles away with a giggle.

I scoot higher on the bed and motion for her to get closer. She settles into my arms, and I bury my nose in her hair. "Santa Day should be fun tomorrow." I trace a pattern over her arms and down her back. "But not as fun as last year."

"Yeah, I don't think anything will ever beat last year's. A first kiss under the mistletoe?" She sits up and out of my arms. "I got you something. It's not your whole Christmas gift, just part of it, but I thought you could have one gift a little early."

I quickly straighten. "Ooh, what is it, what is it, what is it?" I clap my hands.

She goes to the duffel bag she had discarded when she shot through the door and pulls out a rectangle-shaped present not much larger than my hand. She rejoins me on the bed. "Here you go."

I don't waste any time ripping into the paper and producing a frame with the picture of us from last year's Santa Day. Our first picture together, framed. It's so simple, yet so perfect. I can't help the tears that sting my eyes. "I love it," I whisper, avoiding her eyes so she can't see how affected I actually am.

Aracely, like always, knows better. She curls her finger under my chin and lifts my face. "I love you, Eli."

"I love you, too." I trail off slightly and then say, "In love."

She frowns at me, not making sense of what I'm trying to say. "What?"

"I more than love you, Aracely." I lace our fingers together and hold eye contact. "I've fallen so deeply in love with you. I'm still falling. I don't know if I'll ever stop—"

She covers my rambling mouth to silence me. "I'm falling in

love with you, too. I've fallen, and I'm still falling. I don't want it to stop."

"Me either," I reply through her hand.

She smiles and lowers it. "I have one, too. The same picture." She motions to the frame. "That way, we both have a piece of our story even when we're apart."

"The beginning of the story," I add. "The best part. When things are un-muddied with life and circumstances and obstacles."

She laughs. "You're such a writer." She carefully places herself back in my arms and lowers us to the bed. "It's sad that the endings are never perfect." She looks at the picture, still in my hands.

I kiss the top of her head. "Maybe our ending will be perfect. We can be the exception."

She tightens her grip around me. "I hope so, baby. I love you."

"I love you, too."

"You should write a love story. Our love story."

"Maybe I will."

Excerpt from The Stone River Series by Eli Thomas

Book Two: The Oracle

Mason's disappearance has never been fully solved. Although he communicates through various outlets—and his mother swears it's truly him—he is still considered a missing person with a warrant out for his arrest. Some believe he's dead; others believe he's a criminal. Either way, he hasn't been seen since the night of the seance.

Joey managed to get all charges against Abby dismissed before she packed up her life, her niece, and her dignity, then skipped town. Having been possessed by the ancient witch, Gelica, changed and embarrassed her beyond repair. The things she did. The things she said. Joey is certain she'll never be able to save face after that. And she is positive there is no way Sidney will ever forgive her.

Sidney.

The one reason she wanted to stay. She wanted so desperately to tell Sidney she was falling in love with her, but instead, she said good-bye.

Joey glances at Abby in the seat next to her, then turns her eyes back to the road. Abby argued all morning that what they're doing is reckless and stupid. "Why would we go back to the place that broke us both?" she asked this morning.

Joey's grip tightens on the steering wheel. She didn't have an answer. She is really questioning her own sanity at this point. She had a dream, and the dream is telling her what to do. The town is pulling her back. Someone is trying to reach her, and she doesn't know how else to explain it other than that. She knows Sidney will listen and understand...if she's not still angry.

Just past six a.m., exactly two years to the day of Mason's disappearance, Joey and Abby are coming home.

It's eerie to see Stone River so quiet as the sun slowly peeks over the horizon. Joey can only recall the dread and chaos of when she left, including the look on Sidney's face when she realized it was good-bye.

She's so nervous to see her again, Joey thinks she may actually have to pull over and throw up on the side of the road.

Abby groans and stretches. "Are we there?"

Joey sighs. "Yeah." She lazily points at the large town sign sitting at the corner of Highway 15 and County Road F:

Welcome to Stone River
Pop. 8,611
A Place to Call Home!

CHAPTER EIGHT: SILENCE HEALS

The town is reeling over the car accident happening so close to Christmas. Dana is going to pull through, or so I've heard, but it's still something nobody expected the week of Santa Day. Pete warns me that when stuff like this happens, teachers tend to show up to work more for the kids, and I probably won't be needed at the school. Apparently, it's not the students who keep teachers home, it's the education system. I'm offered a sub job at the elementary in a kindergarten classroom to compensate for the lack of ones at the high school, but even in my wildest nightmares, I can't fathom anything more terrifying than being in charge of a group of five-year-olds. My hands shake even as I turn down the offer.

I really need to focus on writing and getting back into the groove of doing my actual job anyway. I have the final book outlined and most of the rough draft written. I just can't find the desire to finish it. There's practically a cult following for my gay leads, Joey and Sidney. I hadn't realized until I really dove deep into the first book that there's also a serious fandom for both witches and 90s pop culture. I combined all three to hit that trifecta, and it has paid off in droves. I'm not sure what my hang-up is exactly. I just can't seem to navigate a way to end the love story. How do I make it a happy ending without making it too obvious or cheeky? Or does that even matter for a romantic storyline? I mean, it's what the readers want. I know it for a fact because I'll occasionally do a deep dive on some message boards that are dedicated to the story. I love seeing the interpretive fan artwork and finding out what readers love or hate.

I can handle just about any criticism, but when the conversations turned into ones of anger over the amount of time between the books, I started distancing myself. I didn't need to add any more guilt to what I was already putting on myself over the time frame and the ending. I'm definitely so far inside my own head that the simple answer is probably the right one: I just can't see it anymore.

Aracely said there was a correlation between Maple Park and Stone River. I'm not naïve; I recognize that part of what I've created is a reflection of me and my experiences. I just don't like being told which parts. But knowing that, how do I write a happy ending for Joey and Sidney when Eli and Aracely barely got a beginning? I spent years and years hung up on a girl who I dated for barely a year and a half. And we were kids at the time. And now, when everything I've wanted to happen with Aracely is actually happening, I feel lost and confused over whether it's the right choice. Either I have issues, or sometimes, love isn't enough.

Rae once said, "Maybe she was the right person, just at the wrong time." I honestly think having heard that helped me heal and start dating again. Believing it was about the timing and not about my own shortcomings made me feel slightly at peace.

I open my computer and crack my knuckles, fully intending to write. I tap a few keys. Type and delete a few sentences. And then stare at the blinking cursor for about four full minutes before gently closing my laptop. So much for groove.

Tommy is at either Tara's or Angie's, I can't remember, and I'm in an empty house. An eerily quiet house. So quiet that I feel like at any moment, Grandma is going to come sidling into the living room from the kitchen and ask me to put away something on a high shelf she can't reach. If I sit still long enough, I swear I can actually hear the kitchen cupboards opening and closing or the squeak of her favorite rocker. If I was a spiritual person, I would think she's haunting me.

While lounging on the couch with Potato and deciding my next move, I glance around the living room. Grandma was a simple person, and she never saw the need to update her furniture or anything if it didn't absolutely need it. She never had much, but she never wanted much, either. I think after my dad died, she lost the only thing she ever wanted to truly keep. Everything else was just fluff.

But I'm not my grandma. I love nice things. I have money. A stupid amount that I enjoy spending. I've been fortunate to have Rae in charge of my contracts. Although Rae would argue it's my talent shining through and making us the money, I think we both deserve the glory.

As if on cue, my phone vibrates, and Rae's face pops up. I've been avoiding her long enough. Time to face it. "Hey, Rae."

"Girl, where have you been?"

"I'm hiding out in my hometown for a few weeks. Until after Christmas, at least."

"Why?" she says with the signature snark I love and people she goes toe-to-toe with hate. "I mean, I know your grandma kicked it, but why are you sticking around when you could be getting back up here? Have you thought more about LA?"

I suck in a shaky breath. She's been nagging me about moving to Los Angeles for almost eight months now. She may have been an integral part of making me money and selling my books, but I also helped her boutique firm skyrocket. She has writers, musicians, actors, and even athletes call and ask for help with contracts and negotiations.

We met in college. She's about eight years older than me, and she was working on campus while trying to pass the bar exam. We are like oil and water, but for some odd reason, it works. "Rae, I don't know if I can do LA right now."

"I know I don't have to explain all the benefits to you again. Please don't make me."

"I already know them all," I reassure her. "We could live together, and I could be an employed writer in the business, and you could get the big clients, and blah blah blah."

"You could start dating some hot girls and get over your ex. You forgot that part."

"The dating sounds nice, but getting over my ex?" I laugh, thinking about the kiss from the other night. "That might take a lobotomy at this point."

"Oh, Jesus, don't tell me."

"Tell you what?"

"You saw Aracely and hooked up, didn't you?"

"No, no, nothing like that. We just kissed a little."

"Ugh. That's worse. Kissing without the sex is just like... love. Gross." I can hear her punching buttons on her treadmill and increasing the speed. I must have stressed her out. "Just go fuck her out of your system, or I'll never get you to LA with me."

I laugh. "I'll consider it."

"Seriously, though, that's not the reason I called. You're never gonna believe who contacted me about you."

"Who?" I start mindlessly playing with my hair and relax a little farther into the couch.

"Netflix."

My fingers pause. "What?"

"Remember that movie script we tried to pitch, but it didn't get anywhere?"

"Painfully well," I say. I spent months converting my first book into a screenplay at her suggestion after she met a few producers. It was harshly rejected about a dozen times. We both gave up on it, and I resigned myself to accepting that I'm not really made out to write for Hollywood. Another reason I'm hesitant to move west. "I sent it to a contact in LA, who pitched it to a producer for Netflix. They want you to turn it into a miniseries."

"Wait, really?" I guess Rae hasn't given up on it like I had thought.

She hums. "And your publisher called. She wants you to write a prequel for a huge advance."

"A prequel?" I frown. "Feels like a money grab. And I'm not even done with the third book."

"Oh, it is. But who doesn't want a little more money?"

"I guess you're right." But the untold truth is, I don't want to do the work for the money. Lining up a prequel with everything that's already established in the series would take a lot of brainpower. A lot of time. A lot of patience. I only have one of three at the moment. "I'll have to get back to you on that one."

"*Okay.*" She draws out the word. "You're kidding, right?"

"What do you mean?"

"I can already tell it's a no. Eli. This is a lot of money."

"I know. I just…I don't know. I just buried my grandma, and things are weird with my mom and brother, and I kissed my ex…I just need some time to think. Some space to think, maybe."

"Or some alcohol," she suggests with a laugh.

"I wouldn't say no to that. I wish you were here to get a drink with me."

"We'll be getting plenty of drinks when we're out in LA." She's crossing a line, and she knows it, but who am I to squash her dreams right now? I know I'm not going to LA, and I know her path is definitely leading her there. We've been in the same city and working together for most of my adult life, and now we're being pulled in different directions. Rae started to mention relocating in her early forties. Now that she's quickly closing in on fifty, I think she feels like if she doesn't do it now, she never will. She doesn't have any close family keeping her in the Midwest, so there's nothing holding her back. Rae is going to end up in LA while I'm starting to feel like I need to be close to home. "I put a copy of the contracts in the mail so you can digest them while you're in Small Town, USA. They should be there today, actually."

"Thanks," I say, genuinely grateful she knows me well enough to know I like paper to scribble on and get frustrated reading contracts on my phone or computer. "When do we meet about Netflix?"

"Soon. So hurry up and find whatever it is you're looking for there and come back to me." I hear a commotion behind her. "Ah, shit. I gotta jet. Love you, boo."

"Love you, too," I respond quietly.

I really need to finish the third book.

❖

I spend the next few days avoiding literally every human on the planet. I turn off the notifications on my phone and just exist with my own thoughts. It's freeing and simultaneously terrifying. I haven't spent much time with just me in so long that I've almost forgotten how to really think and contemplate life. I've definitely forgotten how boring I am.

As promised, the contracts from Rae show up. I barely glance at them before hiding the papers in my bedroom's side attic where Grandma used to store old boxes and decorations. I'll deal with that part of my life either back in Minnesota or after I finish the third book.

I turn my phone back on one morning to order a bunch of new furniture and appliances for Grandma's house and turn it off again while ignoring the notifications that come through. Pushing up my sleeves, I decide to start in the living room with dusting, cleaning out every single space, and moving furniture to clean underneath. With Tommy's permission, I throw out three trash bags and pack four boxes for donation from the living room alone. It's random stuff. Old knickknacks that aren't sentimental, magazines, newspapers, books, lamps, board games, and blankets shoved into every nook and cranny. I vacuum every inch and get on my hands and knees with a bucket to scrub the baseboards. The only part I struggle with is working around the Christmas tree. Tommy will not agree to me taking it down until after Christmas. The carpet needs to be cleaner than just vacuuming, so I go to Wendell's and rent a carpet shampooer.

By the time I haul the thing back to the house, Tommy is there. He's standing in the middle of the living room surveying the progress. I half expect him to chew me out. I hadn't really considered how different it already looks without the old lady clutter. It's more like a living room for a family to exist in now.

"Hey." I test the waters. "I just wanted to get this place clean and—"

He turns, and I stop talking. His eyes aren't angry or sad; they're determined. He gives me a curt nod. "All right then, let's get to work." He unzips his coat and comes to help me haul the shampooer fully into the room. He starts dragging the furniture into the kitchen to really clear space so we can get the carpets nice and clean. I go to the garage and get a ladder so I can dust and scrub every high area. Not a single inch of the living room goes untouched. It's the cleanest this room has been since before either of us lived here. After another hour, we stand back and admire our work. Potato is tentatively watching from a safe distance in the kitchen. We very quickly discovered she is not a fan of the shampooer after she squealed and peed on the edge of the carpet.

"You still have that paint in the garage?" he asks.

I stride to the door before he even has to elaborate. This house has been in desperate need of a makeover for as long as I can remember. Grandma isn't here, so it's my call. Something about that is reassuring. She would want me to follow my instincts and would say something about how I should follow my heart. She left it to me; she wants me to feel like it's my home now. We spend the next four hours laying plastic, taping off, and painting the living room. We paint over the odd green color with a light gray. It makes the entire room so much brighter that it feels bigger somehow. I watch as Tommy puts the finishing touches over the archway leading to the entryway and kitchen. He barely has a drop of paint on him where I have it splattered all over my clothing, arms, and hands. I'm sure there's some on my face, too. As if he senses me watching, he turns and smiles. "Looks good, yeah?"

"It does."

"I've actually been wanting to do this for a while. Sorry I was such a dick about it before."

"No worries. I'm a dick about everything."

"You really are." He laughs and climbs down the ladder. "So," he sighs, "wanna do the entryway and kitchen next?"

"That'll take us all night and tomorrow. Especially since we'll have to take down all the Christmas decorations." I look at the hilariously plastic-wrapped tree in the living room. There are no gifts under it yet. Tommy said the boys' gifts were at their moms' houses, and Grandma hadn't gone shopping for us yet. I'm actually glad for it. Opening a gift from her postmortem would have been too much.

"Is that a no?"

"It's a yes. I'll go get us some caffeine from Pump It. You go get more tape and paint."

"Deal." He sets down his brush. "I'll take a little longer than you, so buy more trash bags and start cleaning out everything like you did in here. I'll hurry, I promise."

"Okay, see you back here soon." I'm actually a little delighted at the chance to spend more time with Tommy. Our silence has been comfortable, and I feel like we're getting so much accomplished. We've never been a conventional family, not even in the way we heal together.

❖

I stroll into Pump It with way more confidence than I had just over a week ago. I'm already more comfortable with the idea of being home. "Hey, Harper," I say as I stride past the counter. I don't even have to look to know she's scrolling through her phone.

"Hey, Thomas." She greets me back through a yawn.

"Slow day?" I ask as I open the drink cooler and pull some bubbly and caffeinated beverages out.

"Mm-hmm. Only three people and now the two of you."

I let the door fall closed. "Two?"

"Me."

The voice is so close, I nearly expire. I spin around, my grip tightening on the bottles. "Aracely," I squeak. "I didn't know you were there."

She smiles, but it's forced. "You've been avoiding me."

"No," I lie. "I've just been busy. Tommy and I are painting and—"

"Don't lie." She calls me on my shit better than anyone.

I sigh and relax my shoulders. "Okay, fine, I was slightly avoiding you."

Harper stands and pretends like she's doing something with the cash register. Guess we're more interesting than whatever she was reading on her phone.

"Because of what I said?"

"No." I adjust the drinks in my arms and walk to the next aisle to grab trash bags.

Aracely follows me. "Eli, I didn't say all of that to make you run. I said it because it's true. It doesn't have to be weird."

"It's not weird," I assure her and shift the drinks to one arm so I can grab a box of bags.

"I don't want to fight about this. I just don't want you avoiding me."

"Aracely." I stop moving and turn. "I'm not avoiding you because of what you said. I'm avoiding everyone, and I do mean everyone, except my brother right now. And even he and I aren't speaking. We're just working on the house. I'm not—"

She surges forward and cuts me off with the force of her hug. "I'm sorry," she whispers. "I shouldn't have taken it personally or made it about me. You're still healing. I'll be here when you're ready."

I don't know what it is about the comfort—if it has to do with the person doing it—but I drop everything and hug her back with such ferocity, I have to actually think to catch my breath. I can feel the tears at bay, but they still don't fall. I want to cry. I want to feel sad. She squeezes me back.

"I can't cry," I confess. "I want to so badly, Aracely. Why can't I cry?"

Somehow, she manages to tighten her grip. "There is no timeline for grief. It'll come when it's meant to."

I slowly pull away, embarrassed at my impulsive confession. I swoop down and pick up the items I dropped. Luckily, nothing broke or exploded. I do a quick glance in Harper's direction. She's openly staring with her face in her hands, completely uninterested in anything else around her. "Jesus, Harper," I whisper.

Aracely doesn't even have to look. "She loves a good daytime soap."

Warmth fills me at the comfort of being with Aracely. "You should come see Potato soon. She could use some healthy attention. I mostly just grunt at her. She pees everywhere and chews everything. She might actually be part gremlin."

"But you love her."

I sigh. "But I love her."

"How about you text me when you're ready for me to come see her."

I'm grateful she's recognizing my need for space. So much is going through my head between losing Grandma, the will, Tommy's kids, Potato, Aracely, my writer's block, even the drama at school, and now the bomb that Rae dropped on me about the miniseries and prequel. I have some decisions to make. Big ones that can take my life in a few different directions.

"So," I lower my voice, "has Harper admitted she's a little bit gay yet?"

We both look at her. As if finally realizing she's staring and attempting to eavesdrop from across the store, she straightens and goes back to her phone.

"Probably," Aracely says. "Plus, I heard she slept with your brother."

"Oh, then she's a lot gay."

She laughs and carefully runs her fingers through my hair. She leans forward to place a soft kiss on my forehead. "Will I see you at Santa Day?" she asks against my skin.

I want to say no. Too many people. Too much past. Instead, I reply with, "Yeah, I'll be there."

❖

It takes Tommy and me most of the next two days to clean out the entire first level of the house, paint, and deep clean. Some of the new furniture arrives early because it was in stock nearby. The look on Tommy's face is priceless when he sees the new recliners and couch. Pure elation.

We load up the old furniture into Tommy's truck and take it to a donation truck parked outside the Legion for the holidays. I finally tell Tommy that I ordered more than just a couch and chairs. Over the next month or so, we'll be getting a new dining room set, new tables for the living room, a new stove, refrigerator, water heater, HVAC unit, windows, bedroom sets and mattresses, carpet, siding, gutters, and roof.

"Eli." He stares at me. "I mean, I knew you had money, but that's a lot."

"I've wanted to update this house for years, Tommy. She never let me do it, and now I have the time and money. Just let me do this. It's helping me." I hadn't even mentioned that I also made arrangements for an electrician, plumber, and builder to come look at the foundation.

His eyes show nothing but understanding. We all heal differently. "Tara and Angie wanna go out for dinner later, and I'm going to T's to watch the boys. You wanna come?"

It's an olive branch. One I gladly accept. "Yeah, I'd really like that."

"What, no joke about them being gay?"

"Oh, I think we both know they're falling in love."

❖

Tommy and I watch the babies without too many hiccups. They've already changed so much in their short little lives that it amazes me. I can see very distinctive traces of my brother in both their faces. Niko inherited more of Tara's dominant genes with her dark skin, hair, and eyes, but he has my brother's tiny round ears. Otis has Tommy's light eyes that pair adorably well with his dark hair. I guess being around them isn't so bad. I kind of like the role of Aunt Eli. I get to spoil them with zero percent of the responsibility of raising them.

When we come home, I hook up Potato and take her for an evening stroll through the streets of my old neighborhood. I haven't truly taken time to enjoy this area of town since being here. I used to go on nightly walks with a group of friends before we were old enough to drive. Occasionally, we rode our bikes, but we mostly just walked. Pete and Tommy were part of that group. Aracely, too, but we rarely spoke to each other until that one Santa Day. Before she became the mother of my nephew, Tara Matthews was also in my friend group. There were a few others sprinkled throughout. Some have moved away or moved on. I'm sure Pete keeps in touch with every single one. He's a good soul like that. They all remind me of Aracely, so I cut everyone out of my life as quickly as I could. Something I gave very little thought to until this extended stay back home. Now I find myself wishing I had more of a connection to a few of my old friends.

As I guide Potato and her short legs down the street and around the first corner, I take some really deep breaths, sucking in as deeply as I can through my nose and releasing out of my mouth. The smell of the cold, the trees, and something palpably Maple Park warms me, despite the biting wind. Most of the people around us have their lights hung. One house a block over has lights synced to dance with the music they're blasting through some old speakers. I can hear it clearly from where I'm standing, and judging by her perked ears, so can Potato.

For a brief moment, I hope the tiny sweater and puppy booties I got her are enough to keep her warm. They were an impulse buy. Not quite as spendy as my other recent purchases but impulsive nonetheless. Potato stops so she can sniff a small snowbank before deciding if she wants to pee on it. I let her explore since this is all new to her and let my head fall back so I can look at the sky. It's really dark already, so I can't see anything until I catch a glimpse of just the tiniest white flecks drifting down and landing on my face.

I watch in wonderment. I've never been looking up at the exact moment it starts to snow; it's truly a sight to behold. I open my mouth as the flakes increase in size and quantity. A few cold drops land on my tongue, and I smile at the childishness of it all. I'm nearly forty and am still taken by the beauty of a fresh snowfall.

I look at Potato, and a laugh bursts past my lips. She's covered in fat snowflakes. "All right," I say. "Let's get back home before you get buried."

❖

On Friday morning, Pete asks me to do one more sub job before winter break. When he tells me it's for Aracely's classroom, I waste no time texting and asking if she's sick. The reply is quick but short. Not sick. Clearly, she's not in the mood to tell me why she's gone, though.

Pete pulls me into his office and hands me a sub folder. "Thanks for doing this on short notice. I'm going to be interviewing a lot of kids today. We figured out the rumors."

My ears perk. "Well, what is it?"

He rolls his eyes. "You won't believe this. A social media trend."

I frown. "Huh?" And I mean that in its entirety. I have no clue how to wrap my head around his explanation.

"A trend that students are doing because of viral videos or something, I don't know." He rubs his eyes. "It's seriously stupid, but the challenge is to start a rumor about a student and a teacher to see who gets in trouble or how big you can get it. Apparently, there was a group of students in Nevada who managed to get a teacher fired and their name printed in the paper before anybody caught on."

"That's sick. Who would do that? We were kids once, too, Pete, but we'd never do something like that."

"The sad thing is, most young people wouldn't. It's the few loud idiots. Anyway, I need to figure out which students are at the bottom of this."

"Who were the victims?"

He gives me a pointed look.

"Okay, fine, you can't tell me."

"No, that's not what that look was. Who are you subbing for today?"

"Aracely?" I can't help the level of my voice as her name practically echoes off the walls. I look around, embarrassed, then whisper, "They tried to say she's having an affair with a student?"

"Yeah." Disappointment is written all over his face. "Hilarious, right?"

"Is she okay?"

"Yes, I just asked her to lay low until after break."

"Who was the student?"

"Who do you think?"

"Ashley Amare."

He nods.

"And Viktor is getting questioned, I presume?"

"Apparently, he was quite offended when Ashley turned him down after he asked her out. I'm going to be sending Ashley home today, too, just to keep her out of the cross fire. She's in Aracely's first period class and usually there before the first bell. Will you tell her? I've questioned her a few times, and she's brought up your name more than once. Apparently, you made an impression in the short time you've known her. She trusts you."

"Yeah, I'll tell her."

"She's not going to want to leave until after her first period. She loves that class. Let her stay if she wants."

"You got it. Anything else?"

He shakes his head. "Nope. Just let me know if you need anything today, and I'll see you tomorrow at Santa Day." He playfully punches my arm.

❖

I walk into Aracely's classroom and am immediately floored by how uniquely decorated it is. She has professional black-and-white pictures of students cooking and baking and working hung all over the classroom. She also has a few color shots of some of the really beautiful foods they've created. There are postings in each kitchen station that give detailed directions on how each appliance, dish, and utensil should be cleaned and returned to its rightful place. On her desk sits a small pencil holder with a tiny Mexican flag sticking out. This room is warm and inviting. No wonder her classes are so popular. I can't believe this is the first time I've come in here.

The first bell of the day hasn't even gone off, and Ashley strides into the classroom. She pauses when she sees me. "Where's Hernandez?"

"She's gone today," I say softly. "And actually, after this class period, Mr. Kelley wants you to go home, too."

I don't know what I expect as a reaction, but it's definitely not the mature nod of understanding she gives. "He figured it out, didn't he?"

"You knew?" I say louder than I want to. I pull the door shut, keeping other students out for the time being.

"Of course I knew. Viktor got all offended when I wouldn't have sex with him. He knew my favorite classes, so he tested out the rumors until something stuck. I was pissed because I really like Ms. Hernandez. The angrier I got, the guiltier I seemed to everyone else, I guess. So I just stayed quiet until Mr. Kelley figured it out."

"You could have talked to me, you know. You saw how I was with Viktor that day. I would have believed you."

"It's not that easy," she argues but with no malice in her voice.

"But it really is that easy," I reply condescendingly. "Just blurt the hard part, and natural conversation will take it from there."

She laughs in my face. "And which part was the hard part? Because I don't even know."

"That you were one of the victims of a social media trend."

She shakes her head.

"I'm serious! Then I would have started asking questions, and it would have come out gradually."

"And what if I said it wrong, and Hernandez took the fall? I didn't want to drag others down."

"Aracely is a big girl. She can handle herself. She would have messed that kid up for you."

Ashley sighs. Her eyes drift off into the distance, and it's almost like she can't make eye contact while she says this next part. "I'm sorry I didn't tell you."

"You don't need to apologize."

"Well, I actually want to thank you."

I frown at her. "For what?"

"For being real with me." She sits at the nearest table and drops her bag on the ground. "Seriously, not many adults take teenagers seriously or give them the time of day. We're just too young and too dumb."

"If the shoe fits."

"Be serious. You do that. Divert with humor."

"Yeah," I say and can't keep the sadness out of my voice. "But, uh, thanks. For saying that. It actually means a lot to hear my time here wasn't a complete waste."

"Nah. You're all right. I figured out where I know you from, too."

"My books?"

"What? No, from Hernandez's desk. She keeps a picture of you in there. What books?"

"I'm an author. What picture? Which drawer?" I stride to Aracely's desk. "And why were you in a teacher's desk?"

Ashley has her phone out and is clearly searching for my name online, ignoring my last question. I eagerly rip open every drawer until I see a small picture frame identical to the one facedown on the nightstand in my bedroom. The picture of us setting up for Santa Day on the night we first kissed. The frame is slightly bulged and popping open in the back. I tip it to see if something is broken inside but catch a glimpse of green. Hands shaking, I pop the back off and see a small sliver of fake mistletoe and a tiny purple ribbon. I look back in the drawer and see that she has been working on a letter to me. I flip through the pages of the notepad. There are about eight drafts of the same thing. She's sorry she didn't follow me. She's sorry she pushed me away for money, and yet she's not sorry because I accomplished what I needed. She's never found what we had with anybody else. She wants me and only me. It basically reiterates over and over what she finally had the courage to say to me in the locker room earlier this week.

Ashley breaks into my thoughts. "Holy shit, you're a legit

author. I'm buying these books right now. I have my mom's credit card saved."

I take a deep breath and slowly release it, still torn between whether I let Aracely back in or take the growth I've made and finally move on with some closure. I'm not made for this town anymore, I know that.

But I think I may still be made for the girl.

The night before Santa Day, twenty-one years ago

A requirement for being on the varsity basketball team is that every year, both the boys' and girls' teams have to assist at the Legion the night before Santa Day. We help with setup, snacks, decorations, the works. When I walk into the Legion, I see Pete and another guy blowing up balloons and taking full advantage of the helium. Across the large room, a group of girls and guys flirt with one another and throw decorations rather than hang them up. The entire scene actually annoys the hell out of me. Not only because I have zero interest in flirting with boys, but because my grandma takes Santa Day really seriously, I do, too. I hate that we need chaperones here to get anything done because the majority of the team just screws around.

"Thomas," Pete yells at me with a high-pitched helium voice. "Coach assigned you to the back room. You're making the goody bags again."

I tip my head at Pete to confirm that I heard him. When I get to the back room, fully expecting to be alone, I almost collapse from shock when I see Aracely Hernandez already back there with a system in place for her bag stuffing. "Oh," I say. "Hi."

"Hi," she responds, looking at me with the same amount of surprise. "I didn't think anybody would be back here with me."

"I didn't think anybody would be back here with *me*. I've done this job alone for the last two years."

"Well, I didn't make varsity until this year." She smiles. "We're not all superstars, you know."

I smile back and immediately feel insecure when my face gets warm. I'm not great at taking compliments. It's even worse when it's coming from a girl who is as gorgeous as Aracely. We've been in the same friend group through most of middle and high school, but we've never really talked beyond casual conversation around the lunch table. We've certainly never been alone. "So." I motion to the folding tables piled with snacks and empty brown paper bags. "What system do you have going here?"

I can hear her sigh of relief and look at her questioningly. She waves off my frown. "I thought you were going to say that you've already done this and have your own system. I just got this all worked out, and I may have cried if you mocked or changed it." She releases a shaky laugh. "And now I'm rambling. I'm sorry. You do that to people, you know. Make them nervous."

I point to myself. "Me? I make people nervous?"

"You're the star basketball player and straight A student. It's really intimidating. Especially—"

"I rarely even talk—" I interrupt and talk over her.

"Because you're so pretty—"

"And I'm kind of an asshole."

"And funny."

"Wait, what?"

"And you don't..." She trails off. Her cheeks turn red.

"Did you just call me pretty?" I'm flattered and nervous but also convinced she's made a mistake. I glance at myself. Sweatpants and an old hoodie. And they're both different shades of gray. I know my hair is in a messy ponytail, and I have flyaways coming out in every direction. I didn't bother with any makeup today, and I'm fairly certain I rubbed my eyes raw before coming here because I'm so tired from staying after practice to get a few more shots in. Actually, I'm perplexed by how put together she looks after having been at the same practice as me. She obviously went home and cleaned up.

"I did," she responds slowly. "I mean, it can't be the first time you've heard that."

It is the first time I've heard it from someone other than a parent or grandparent, but I don't mention it. "It's just weird coming from someone who looks like you." Her eyes bulge, and I realize that probably sounded offensive. "Someone who has all the attention from literally every guy in school," I say quickly. I can't stop my eyes from trailing up her body. She's in cute fuzzy boots layered over skinny jeans and an oversized red sweater that flows in the right places and hugs in better ones. Her hair is down, big, and curly. She has just the slightest amount of makeup that makes a person wonder if she's actually wearing any or is just that beautiful naturally. "Did you really go home from practice and shower for this?"

"Yes, I did. And I don't care about any attention from boys. I think maybe we have that in common." She winks, finding her confidence, and I nearly swallow my own tongue.

"So, um, this system." I motion to the table again.

"Oh!" She claps her hands. "You start at this end with the brown bags and work left to right. Two handfuls of peanuts, one handful of chocolate candies, an apple, and a Wendell's coupon in each bag. Roll the top and pile them into the big box down there. We have about five hundred to make because each kid gets one after sitting on Santa's lap. Then we have to get out the box of mistletoe to hang some up here. There aren't many left to choose from."

I grin at her hopeful expression when she turns to me. "Thanks," I finally say. "Let's get to work." I grab a bag and start to stuff it with peanuts and candy. "Why is there a disposable camera back here?" I motion to the tiny yellow thing lying in the middle of the table in an attempt to keep the conversation going. Typically, I'd be wishing for peace and quiet and alone time, but being here with her isn't so bad. I think I may actually like the company.

She rolls up her first full bag the same time I do. We deposit them into the box and start the process all over again. "They want us to take pictures of the setup process for some slideshow or something. Want me to take your picture?"

"Hell no."

"How about I take one of both of us?" She grabs the camera and pulls me closer. She attempts to center the front of the camera to get us in the frame. "Ready? Are you smiling?" I press my face closer to hers and smile. I can feel her smile against my cheek. She clicks the picture, and I step back into my spot to continue filling bags. We fall into a comfortable silence for a moment before she clears her throat. "So how come we don't really talk? Like, without our friends around?"

"I'm not sure," I answer honestly. "I'm not very social. I don't know how I ended up with a group of friends. I don't really like being around a lot of people."

"Why is that?"

"I don't know. I just feel more comfortable when I'm alone."

"Do you want me to leave you alone?"

"No," I say quickly and loudly.

She jumps and drops an apple.

"I'm sorry," I say much quieter. "I didn't mean for that to come out so aggressively."

She laughs at herself, retrieves the apple, and starts to close her second bag. She sighs when she watches me go back to the far end of the long table and start the process again. "We've only made four bags."

"Four hundred ninety-six to go."

"Do you have a better system?" She cocks an eyebrow, almost like a challenge.

"I might have an idea of a way we can speed this up. Less movement for each of us and kind of like an assembly line."

"Why didn't you just say it from the start?"

"You were so proud. I didn't want to take that away."

She laughs. "You shit," she says with a flirty tone. "Okay then, explain this assembly line."

I clear my throat and attempt to hide my building bashfulness. "I will stand on this end of the table and be in charge of bags, peanuts, and chocolate. I'll put all the bags I fill here," I motion to the center of the table, "and you'll take over with apples, coupons, and rolling. Then"—I move around her and pull the big box for the finished products closer to her legs—"you just toss them in here. Nothing will break, just throw and go. We'll probably get twenty done in the time it took us to do four."

She looks at her watch. "Okay, you're on. Moving at normal speed, let's see how many we can make. I'll be the timer."

"I love a healthy competition." I bump my hip to hers.

She waits for the minute to change and says go. We spend the next several minutes working through the system I set up. To her credit, she doesn't try to slow down or cheat in order to prove me wrong. We genuinely work in tandem, albeit very quietly.

"Okay, time," she says.

"How many are there?" I motion to the box.

She bends down and counts. "Not twenty."

"Damn." I snap my fingers.

"Twenty-two."

I put both my fists in the air. "Victory."

She stands. "Yeah, yeah. Okay, let's keep going. But can we talk while we work?"

"Yes, please," I practically beg.

We both get back to business. It takes a minute or so before she actually asks me a question. "Why aren't you talking?"

"I was waiting for you," I answer honestly. "I'm not great at small talk. Remember? I don't know how I have friends." I laugh.

"I think your brother helped you out there. He's pretty vocal."

"Oh God, did Tommy hit on you?"

She laughs. "No, no nothing like that. I'm just saying he's very personable and tends to draw in a crowd. I think you just gained notoriety by association."

I shrug. "Probably."

She rolls the tops of two bags and tosses them in the box. "So, Eli," she begins slowly, "what do you wanna do after you graduate?"

My stomach tightens in a satisfying way at her use of my first name. Most people associated with me and the basketball team just call me Thomas. "I…" My voice wavers slightly. "I think I want to be a writer."

She must have noticed my nerves bubbling to the surface. "Has nobody ever asked you that before?"

I shake my head. "My grandma and my school counselor. That's about it." I crack my knuckles to shake off some of the anxiety at being vulnerable in front of a girl I am quickly developing a crush on. "And Ms. Bonnie told me I should be a writer, so I guess I kind of told her after that."

"She was my favorite English teacher."

"Mine too." I breathe in and relax a bit. Aracely isn't being judgmental or unkind. I honestly feel like I can be more open with her in this moment. "I just haven't really opened up about it to anyone because people tend to criticize those with big dreams, you know?"

She nods. "Yeah, they do. Try having a Latina parent." She laughs. "Work hard and make money, that's the measure of success."

I don't say anything, realizing I don't know much about Aracely, and I certainly don't know anything about growing up as the child of a first-generation immigrant. "So what do you want to do?"

"Make money, I guess." She laughs it off, but I can tell it's something that actually weighs heavily on her. When I remain quiet, she continues, "There was a time when my mom had it really rough. We both did, I guess, I just don't remember it as well. She had to leave a bad situation, and when that happens, money is literally the only goal."

I nod. "Yeah, that makes sense."

"So how will you become a writer? I don't even know where one begins with that."

"I'm hoping I will earn some scholarships for grades and sports to college, where I'll get into a writing program and write a bestseller."

She attempts to push her unruly hair behind her ears. "That's quite the reach."

"It's the only goal I've ever had. I'm not sure I can picture anything else."

"No backup plan?"

I shrug. "Maybe something in the medical field?"

"But you don't find any passion in that."

I'm clearly not the only observant one.

"Can I read some of your writing?"

I pause. "You have. In class."

"I've read what you've written for assignments when we do peer edits in English. That's not the same. I want to read something you've written for leisure. Something you wrote because you wanted to write it."

"That's scary," I say without thinking. I've never shared my personal writing with anybody before.

"A little bit." She nods. "But that's being a writer."

I swallow hard. "I guess you can call me Dr. Thomas, then."

She bumps my shoulder. "I can help you practice talking in front of people."

"You definitely could give me some pointers. It's pretty impressive that you've been announcing the Memorial Tree since sixth grade." The lighting of the Memorial Tree is one of my grandma's favorite traditions on Santa Day, so she has me and Tommy watch with her every year. There's always a light on it for my dad and grandpa.

"I was really nervous at first. It's gotten easier, and the names don't change a whole lot from year to year," she admits.

"You never answered what do you want to do after high school."

"That's because I'm not sure yet. Something with food, I think. I really love cooking. It brings people together."

I slow my movements and smile at her.

She turns and meets my eyes. "What?" She laughs nervously. "Oh God, do I have something on my face?"

"No." I laugh. "That was just a really good answer."

Her cheeks color slightly. "Plus," she continues nervously, "it's something I can do where there will always be employment because there will always be restaurants, and people will always need to be fed." I'm beginning to see how integral money has been as a stressor and motivator in her life. "Oh shoot." She snaps her fingers, effectively breaking my train of thought. "We need to unpack the remaining mistletoe and hang them up so we can spray them with the cinnamon scent."

"Oh, okay, I'll grab them." I stop packing bags and move to the other side of the table to open up one of the boxes marked "Maple Park Mistletoe." I flip open the box and find the reject mistletoes smashed into the bottom of the box. "Oh, jeez, these are some sad toes."

Aracely walks around the table to join me. She peeks inside as I tip the box. "Bummer. We can try to liven them up a bit. Just a little TLC is all they need." She squeezes my arm and reaches in for the fake green leaves messily strewn about the bottom of the box.

"They never get replaced. At least, that's what my grandma says. She told me last year that the fake mistletoes that are hung all around town are the same ones from when she was in elementary school the year Santa Day started." She hands me one, and I start to bend and peel the wired stems to get them to look a little more alive. "They just get sprayed with cinnamon and rehung. The same plastic and wire year after year."

"What a weird thing to be cheap on. Why not just buy new ones?"

I shrug. "I suppose it made sense at the time to reuse them, and now it's a problem for next year every year."

"You're probably right. They're not labeled or anything, so different ones get strung up in different places, huh?"

I frown. "Um, I guess so. Why?"

"We should mark one. See where it ends up every year, and only the two of us will know."

"Might end up in the bar."

"Or at Wendell's."

"The school."

"Post office."

"Back here in the Legion."

"Or on one of the outside poles."

I bump her shoulder this time. "I like it. Let's do it. This could go on for years before someone bothers to notice."

"Okay!" She bounces in place, and I stand there like a smiling buffoon, wondering what it would be like to kiss her. The urge to push my fingers through her hair and pull her in by the belt on her jeans takes over my entire being. "How should we mark it?" She breaks into my thoughts.

"Um, how about ribbon?" I push the thoughts of kissing her out of my mind as much as I can. We're in the same friend group. I don't want to make things weird for everyone.

"Oh, good idea. There's some ribbon in the other back room that's left over from wrapping presents. I'll go grab it." Before I even have a chance to respond, she drops the mistletoe into my arms and practically runs out of the room.

I carefully examine the options we have, and it looks like the one I had originally started with may be the best option. One of them is actually in pieces and being held together by duct tape. I pull a folding chair to the doorway of the back room and climb on top. Carefully, I run my fingers along the top of the door frame, looking for the tiny telltale hook that was put there for the wire. Once I find it, I slip the loop over and stretch it out until the mistletoe is firmly planted in the middle of the door frame.

"Here you go," comes from below me. I look down and see Aracely with her big brown eyes and delicate hand stretched in my direction, holding a piece of purple ribbon. "I figured the purple will be easy to spot anywhere. It'll really stand out."

"I love it." I take the ribbon and gently tie it into a tight bow around the top of the mistletoe and carefully cut the ribbon so it's even and looks like it was always meant to be there.

"There," I say as I jump off the chair. I land on the side of Aracely's foot and lose my balance.

Her arms go around my waist to steady me as I drop the scissors and the ribbon. "Whoa, there." Her grip tightens as I find my footing. "You okay?" she whispers.

It's then I realize how close our faces are.

I nod slowly. My eyes drift up for a millisecond, but it's enough for her to catch me doing it. Her eyes follow.

We're standing under the mistletoe.

I'm about to apologize profusely and pull away until she leans forward. It's just enough to invite me to come the rest of the way.

I swallow and close my eyes, ready to be brave, but I don't have a chance. Apparently, she's tired of waiting. She closes the gap quickly and lets out a shaky breath between our lips when my hands go straight to her hair. I trace her neck and tilt my head so I can deepen the kiss. She leans forward again, and my knees nearly give out as her tongue swipes my bottom lip. Just as I open my own mouth, a voice makes me jump so high, it feels like my skin is going to come off my body.

"Holy shit."

We both step away from one another and look. Pete. And that other guy.

"Sorry, I didn't mean to interrupt," Pete says quickly. "I was looking for scissors."

I shift nervously and point to the floor where I dropped them.

"Oh, right," he says.

He scoops them off the floor and grabs the other guy by the shirt to pull him away from us as he's saying, "Dude, those girls were kissing."

I turn back to Aracely, petrified that a line has been crossed. Not only have we kissed, but someone had seen it and that could—

My thoughts are cut off by the ferocity of her second kiss. This time, there's no hesitation. It's all tongues, lips, heavy breathing, hands everywhere. When she pulls back, I have to blink a few times to catch myself. "Sorry," she breathes out. "I just wanted to finish what we started."

"I did, too," I say, breathless.

She smiles and looks at her feet. "Maybe we could do that again? Like, after a date or something?"

I nod so quickly my cheeks bounce before I realize she's still looking down. "Yes," I say loudly. She jumps. "Sorry," I whisper. "Yes. Please, let's do that."

Her smile grows to the point that I can see all of her teeth. It's so endearing that I step forward and peck her on the cheek before bending to scoop up the remaining piece of ribbon. I walk to the table where I left the broken pieces of mistletoe and tie the small ribbon around one of the pieces. "Here." I hold out the miniature version of the mistletoe we just kissed under. "Happy Santa Day."

She takes the offering, her hands shaking. I can't tell if she's nervous or touched or something else. "Thank you," she says, quietly. "Can I kiss you again?"

Instead of answering, I step forward, wrap my arms around her waist, and lean in.

CHAPTER NINE: SANTA DAY

After school, I head home hoping to find Tommy still working on cleaning out the upstairs bedrooms. Instead, I see Mom's car in the driveway. I groan with frustration but don't delay going into the house.

Tommy and Mom are in the living room with the babies. They both turn when I walk in, but neither make a move to get up. "The boys are here," Tommy calls excitedly. "They're coming to Santa Day tomorrow."

"That's great, Tommy. How far did you get on the upstairs?"

"Eleven trash bags. Three to the dumpster and the rest to donation. But that's enough until after Christmas."

"After Christmas? Jesus, what are we doing for the next three days?"

"Eli. *Christmas*," he reiterates and frowns at me like I'm Ebenezer Scrooge.

"Here we go," Mom chimes in. I knew it wouldn't take long to get her input. "Always the same with her."

"Oh, there you are, Teri. Almost thought I was seeing a mirage since you hadn't insulted me yet."

"Eli, stop, please," Tommy begs.

"I'm just trying to enjoy time with my grandsons in this very impressive display of money." She motions to all the new furniture. "I knew you had a lot, but I didn't realize you had enough for this."

"I wanted to update the house. It needs a makeover," I say simply.

"Hope you don't expect Tommy to pay you back." She tickles under Niko's chin and coos at him.

A sharp pang hits my chest. This display of tenderness and care used to be directed at Tommy and me. There's still a piece of the old her in there. The loving mother, who is now a grandmother.

"Why would I do that to him?" I ask, genuinely insulted she even insinuated I would.

Tommy throws his hands up and announces he's leaving if we can't get along. He manages to get both boys into his arms and walks into the dining room where the bassinets are set up. I can hear him shushing them and ignoring us.

I look at the tiny dog bed next to the fireplace and see Potato curled into a ball, asleep. She has a sweater on, which tells me that Tommy took her out. For a moment, I feel terrible that my mother and I can't get along long enough to allow my brother to enjoy time with his kids in his own home.

"You've been home less than five minutes and already upset your brother," she bites as she moves to sit in one of the new recliners.

I stand there, unmoving, trying to decide if I should hold my ground and keep bickering with her or go apologize to Tommy.

"Eli," Mom says quietly before I have a chance to decide. "I'm sorry about the other day."

There's the apology I was expecting in a text. I love that she's willing to admit wrongdoing, but I hate that it never makes her change her actions. I sigh, defeated. I guess my decision was made for me. "Me too."

I don't apologize to Tommy and instead run up the stairs two at a time to get to my bedroom. I always feel awkward after those weird interactions with my mom and feel the need to put some distance between us. I lie on my old bed for a while before changing into a hoodie and jeans and attempt to sneak down the stairs.

"Where are you going?" Tommy asks as I head to the door.

Busted before I could make a clean getaway. "The game. It's the only home game I'll catch while I'm still in town. I wanna see what this new coach is doing with the team. I'll be back later."

"Oh, okay," he says with such sadness that I actually feel guilt coursing through my body.

I pause. "I can't wait to see the boys in their outfits at Santa Day. I know they'll be the cutest babies there."

He offers a half-smile. "See you then."

The hurt digs a little deeper. Tommy actually wants to spend time with me. We're finally mending whatever has been broken between us, and here I am, running away because I don't want to be near my mom for fear of us fighting again.

I hesitate for half a second as I reach for the yellow peacoat I've grown to love and officially claim as my own.

I need a break. I need fresh air.

Tommy can wait.

If I thought that walking back into the high school office was a tidal wave of nostalgia, walking into a high school basketball game is a tsunami. The smell of fresh popcorn is what hits me first. My mouth waters immediately. Second is the sound. Shoes squeaking on the gym floor, the chatter of the crowd, the bright lights, and the general feeling of excitement coming from every corner of the small gymnasium.

Pete spots me standing in the doorway of the home side seating and waves me over. I climb the bleachers quickly and plant myself next to him.

He looks me over, and I squirm slightly under the examination. "Rough day?"

"It was fine until I got home and saw my mom."

"Oh. Gotcha." He doesn't press for more. I can't blame him for not knowing what to say. None of my friends have ever known anything about my relationship with my mother except Aracely. "How did Ashley take it this morning when you sent her home?"

"She was perfect, like you predicted."

"Yeah, I figured. Viktor rolled on a few other kids in a matter of minutes. He cried a lot. He's suspended for now. We're having a parent meeting to decide next steps. Of course, Aracely doesn't want to press charges."

"She should," I say matter-of-factly.

"I agree." He leans back on the row behind us, and I follow suit. "But I can't force her."

"I'm glad he cried."

"Me too." He releases a laugh of what seems to be relief. "It shows that he has regret and some compassion left in him."

"That's not the reason I'm glad." I frown at him. "I want him to hurt."

He releases a long breath. "Well, yes, I suppose that's the popular opinion, but we can't punish people forever for the mistakes they make as teenagers. He's still just a kid. His brain is still developing, and he's learning life's boundaries." Pete looks at me, and when I refuse to meet his eyes, he continues. "He's showing remorse, and I'm guessing this will be a pivotal moment that determines the type of man he grows into." He waits for me to respond again, but I remain stoic. "I mean, are you the same person you were at seventeen? Or did you grow and evolve as you learned the ways of the world?"

That statement knocks all the air from my chest. It hurts to suck in my next breath. "You're right," I whisper. I watch the girls' basketball team finish their warm-ups and circle up for a final huddle before game time. "I guess I was kind of in the wrong."

"No, you weren't. What Viktor did was absolutely horrendous. He'll be punished for it, but hopefully, he will make better choices moving forward. Sorry, I didn't mean to get all philosophical on you." He stretches his arms and brings his hands to a rest behind his head right as the jump ball is thrown to signal the beginning of the game.

I watch the game slowly unfold, and I vaguely hear Pete explaining how they have a lot of talent coming up the ranks for the next few years, but I'm not paying attention. My mind is a million miles from the present day, planted firmly in the past. Aracely had said something similar about a mistake she made at eighteen. Pete wasn't talking directly to me, but it couldn't have been more relevant. I'm punishing Aracely for a mistake she made as a kid when she thought she was doing the right thing. I'm holding a lot of grudges, including one against Grandma for this whole will ordeal.

I sit quietly and watch the game, occasionally nodding along with what Pete says until halftime. The Trojans are up by over twenty. It's pretty obvious where this game is headed, so I politely excuse myself and leave the gymnasium. The trip down memory lane is great, but kind of like Pete said, I've outgrown this part of my life. It's a chapter I closed a long time ago, and I'm okay with that. I'd rather focus on the parts that need more resolution.

I go back to Grandma's house, let Potato out one last time, and head to bed. My room looks different than when I last saw it, and it makes me pause for a moment. It seems like someone has been in here rummaging around because things are just the slightest bit different from when I left. I frown and look at Potato. "You been going through my things?"

She rolls to her back, asking for her tummy to be rubbed. I stoop and give a few pats. "All right, chunk, let's go to bed." I quickly change into some pajamas, lift Potato to the bed, turn off my phone, and turn out the lights.

❖

Santa Day is already in full swing by the time I step outside the next morning. There are people walking down the street to see the parade, and Potato is losing her ever-lovin' mind barking at them. I had let her out in the backyard and then quickly decided this is a good day for her to stay home. Santa Day may be too much for her little nerves. I block her in the kitchen area with some chew toys, water, and a little bit of food. I know I'll be cleaning up piss and shit when I get home, but it's okay as long as I know she's comforted and safe. For a brief moment, I wonder when I transitioned from a skeptic who wanted nothing to do with a puppy to the protective dog mom I'm currently being.

I make quick work of getting down the street to see the parade route. It goes from Pump It at the far end of town, down Main Street, and concludes near the Legion and the park where they light the memorial tree. I've seen the creative winter- and holiday-themed floats so many times, and they still amaze me. There are some seriously creative people and businesses in this small town. As I walk along, I spot the high school dance team doing a rendition of "Jingle Bell Rock" while dressed as Christmas trees. It's both ridiculous and impressive. My favorite float has always been by the family who owns the orchard and pumpkin patch just outside town. Every year, they do some sort of fruit theme and hand out candied produce. When I spot their float just ahead, my legs grow a mind of their own and actually start to jog and then run to catch up. I'm dodging little kids, elderly couples, pets, and ice patches. A different version of me would be rolling her eyes and embarrassed, but something powerful has taken over my body. Once I get a good distance ahead of the float, I dive past the row of watchers and stand on the curb, waving my hands in the air just like those around me.

I make eye contact with one of the float runners who is going back and forth from the wagon to the street and smile to let her know I need whatever she's handing out. It works. She tosses me a small gossamer bag that is freezing cold to the touch. Whatever they're throwing is being kept in a cooler and is just as cold as the air outside. When I open the bag, I see why. It's four black gold cherries dipped in a chocolate shell. I'm sure they were frozen through the summer just for this event.

Wasting no time, I pull one clean from the stem with my teeth. I don't even try to stop my moan as I bite down and feel the cold chocolate crack and the freezing cherry juice coat my tongue. Just as the dark chocolate starts to melt, a voice from behind me pulls my attention.

"Wow. I'm a little jealous those cherries can do that much for you." Aracely looks positively adorable in her knit cap and puffy winter coat. She laughs, and I watch the puff of air leave her lips and evaporate into the air around her.

"Have you tried these? You'd lose yourself, too." I offer her my small bag.

She holds up a hand, stopping me. "Please, I've already had two bags. I'm not an amateur."

"I'm definitely not sharing, then."

"Are you headed to the lighting of the memorial tree?"

I make my way back to the sidewalk with Aracely in tow. "Yeah, I was going to see how Grandma's kringla turned out."

"Oh, it's still amazing but nothing compared to hers. I think she left an ingredient off the recipe card just so nobody could completely recreate the magic. Not even a trained chef."

"She was clever that way." I think of the will and my untouchable Starfire. Clever indeed. "I'm sure you did a spectacular job. I can't wait to try it." Suddenly, something dawns on me. "So you did stick with the culinary science major at Iowa State?"

"I did. That's why I was able to get endorsed as a family and consumer science teacher. I already had the professional accolades."

"Did you still double major like you planned?"

"I sure didn't." She smiles at me. "I actually took a few journalism classes and a photography class. I was trying to find another niche but ended up graduating before anything else stuck." We start walking in the direction of the Legion. I remain quiet and soak up the fact that I'm starting to fill in the pieces of Aracely I had been missing. "Is it okay that I'm coming with you?" she asks after a prolonged silence.

"Yes, of course." I pause again. "Did you ever work as a chef?"

"I was a sous chef at a downtown restaurant for a few years, but I hated it. I was at a bakery for almost four years. I was just about to quit when Mom got sick. Of all my jobs, I have actually enjoyed teaching others how to bake, cook, and maintain proper kitchen etiquette the most. Education is a terrible field, though. Actually"—she laughs to herself—"I've been reading about all of these traveling food reviewers and trying to figure out how to get one of those jobs. Seems like a perfect fit for me."

"Yeah, it does." In fact, I can't imagine a more perfect role for Aracely. "Does it pay well?" I ask.

She looks at me, probably trying to gauge if I'm being genuine or snide since money was a reason for our breakup. I do my best to give her the sincerest look I can manage and show that I hold no animosity anymore.

"Well," she says slowly, "it actually pays close to nothing." A humorless laugh bubbles past her lips. "Took me a while, but I think I learned that money isn't as important as I once thought."

"I—"

"I'm sorry if I ever made you feel like money was more important than you. Than us."

The words I've wanted to hear for so, so long. My heart beats hard under my coat, and my throat goes dry. I think of the letters I saw in her desk. It took a lot for her to say those words.

"I forgive you, Aracely." I stop walking for a moment and turn. "I'm sorry, too. For making you the villain when you were just making the choice you thought was best." We start walking again. Silence hangs between us, like we're both too scared to break whatever truce we just reached. I'm the first who is brave enough to speak again. "Coming from someone who has a decent amount of money, it doesn't make me happy. So that mystery is solved."

She laughs. "I don't know," she says in a singsong. "It makes you less stressed, therefore probably happier."

I smile. "I suppose you're correct." I bump my shoulder to hers. "Can't kiss money, though."

"I would."

I bark a laugh. I guess neither of us can fully let go of what we learned as kids. We're just about to reach our destination when I have a full body shiver. "How long until Santa arrives? I might need to go inside BJ's and warm up."

"There's hot chocolate sponsored by Alma just ahead. And"— she turns and points—"he's on the fire truck right there."

I glance over my shoulder to see Santa Claus riding on top of the colorfully lit fire truck ambling our way. Santa has a bullhorn up to his mouth, but I can't quite hear him yet. Muscle memory tells me he's repeating the phrase, "Happy holidays, Maple Park!" over and over.

"Perfect. Now walk me to the hot chocolate." I loop my arm through her elbow. "This can be our coffee rain check."

I feel her stiffen for a split second, then relax against me. She puts her head on my shoulder. "Gladly."

As we reach the hot chocolate stand, there are already kids ditching the end of the parade to start on the snowman building contest in the giant empty lot next to the Legion. Tommy and I tried that contest for six years straight before we relinquished it to the next generation of builders. We never won. The highest honor we were able to achieve was third place, and that was our very first year. Grandma told us it was beginner's luck.

I bump Aracely. "Did you ever win the snowman building?"

She looks positively offended. "Of course I did. Twice."

"Can't believe I didn't know that."

She pinches my side playfully. "You should remember. I beat you and Tommy both times."

"Ah," I say, it all becoming so clear. "I was far too busy pouting about our loss to ever pay any attention to who actually won."

"I still have the trophies if you wanna kiss them later."

"Fun-ny," I enunciate, "but no thanks, showboat."

I glance around as we inch closer to the front of the hot chocolate line. The atmosphere of Santa Day hasn't changed a single bit in all the years I've experienced it. It's always cold, and everybody is always so delighted. It's almost like the excitement overpowers the weather.

As I scan the festivities and crowd, I notice the memorial tree is all strung up and ready to go. There's a makeshift wooden stage next to it with a microphone and speaker system hooked up and ready to go for Santa. He always ends the parade, opens for the tree lighting, and then closes by letting kids sit on his lap for hours on end.

A *whoop whoop* noise pulls the attention of everyone to the far end of the street where a fire truck inches into a parking spot near the Legion. The parade is ending just as we get to the front of the table.

"Two hot chocolates, please," Aracely practically sings.

"Here you go, my dear." She's handed two steaming cups by

a smiling volunteer. "Toppings bar to the right. Enjoy, and merry Christmas."

"Happy holidays to you, too," Aracely says back and motions me to the toppings table. She's always so careful about not assuming people's holidays, but she does it with such grace that nobody ever realizes she's correcting them. I, on the other hand, am awful about it. I've always been in awe of how kindly she instills good behavior in others. We used to balance each other out in that sense.

A round of applause echoes through the cold air, and I don't even have to turn my head to know that Santa and the truck have officially parked, and he's making his way to the stage.

"Peppermint?" Aracely asks.

"Huh?" I turn to her.

"You always used to put just peppermint in your hot chocolate. Still the same?"

I blush slightly. "Um, yes. Good memory."

"Do you remember what I get?"

"Everything you can possibly fit into the cup," I say with confidence.

"Ding, ding, ding." She leans into me as she starts dutifully scooping chocolate chips, peppermint, candy, sprinkles, whipped topping, and extra syrup into her cup.

"That makes my teeth hurt."

"Oh, shut it. I only do this once a year."

I suck in a nervous breath before finally asking, "Have you heard anything about the student in the accident? Dana?"

Her smile falls. "She's going to be okay, but it's going to be a long healing process. Her family has an online fund that was started by some of their friends. It's going to be a lot of physical therapy and adjusting their house for a wheelchair."

I make a mental note to donate to the fund later.

A booming voice over the speakers near us stops the conversation. "Ho, ho, ho! Happy holidays, Maple Park!" People cheer, and a crowd quickly forms near the stage. The people who were watching the parade know to follow the fire truck at the end, so the space has filled up considerably.

I'm staring at the giant evergreen and lights strung all about, comfortable inside this crowd of familiar faces, when I realize that this has always been my favorite part of the season. And I've missed out on it for years. It was Grandma's favorite, too. A pang of hurt shoots through my chest as I recall the number of times she called and asked me to come back for Santa Day, only for me to disappoint her. I make a silent promise to myself that I'll come back in the coming years to see my nephews and experience this as many times as possible. Being here and seeing people is not nearly as awful as I made it out to be in my mind.

"Happy Santa Day," he bellows into the mic and gets a lot of feedback. People throw their hands up to their ears but still manage to cheer for him. Santa continues to work the crowd by asking for cheers or jeers of those who have been naughty or nice.

Just then, something dawns on me. "Aracely?"

"Mm?" she responds around her drink.

"Do you still announce the memorial tree?"

She looks at me over the rim of her cup. "Wanna come onstage with me?"

"Hell no." But I can't stop the smile. She's been in this role since her grandfather passed when we were in elementary school.

As if on cue, Santa says, "I'd like to welcome Aracely Hernandez to the stage to lead the annual tree lighting ceremony."

"Be right back."

There's applause from the crowd, and a path forms to lead her up to the stage. In less than a minute, she is the star of the show. She steps to the mic. "Good morning, everyone, and welcome back to Maple Park's annual Santa Day celebration. First, allow me to run through today's planned activities. We'll start with the yearly tree lighting, then all children are welcome to sit on Santa's lap in the Legion—"

"Hey." A voice pulls my attention. Tommy.

"Hey," I say, genuinely glad to see him. I look at the double stroller and can't see anything because it's covered so tightly for warmth. "Where are the moms?"

"They're going inside to get us a front spot for the boys to sit on Santa's lap." He motions to the stroller. "It's empty. I just wanted to hear the reading of the names."

He wants to hear *Dad*'s name. Another thing I've missed to add to the ever-growing list. More and more, my reasons for avoiding this place are getting less and less powerful, and owning the Starfire has become something of a distant memory.

Aracely continues to instruct the crowd. "Feel free to head into BJ's for a free-donation buffet line. It'll be open from now until four o'clock. As always, BJ promised to serve drinks at a discount rate for all the stressed-out adults this holiday season."

The crowd laughs, and I shake my head. She knows how to charm anyone and everyone.

"My late grandfather started the tree lighting tradition over fifty years ago to honor the loved ones of Maple Park residents who have passed away. Grandpa always said that you feel the people you've loved and lost the most during the holiday season. He wanted to give everybody a chance to dedicate a piece of the holiday back to the dearly departed as a reminder that they still glow in our hearts. Each bulb on the tree represents a name on the list, and the star on top is dedicated in loving memory of my grandfather, Larry Hernandez."

The crowd claps. Tommy leans over to me. "This is always my favorite part. Other than building a snowman."

I look at him, but his attention is on the stage as Aracely pulls some papers from her pocket. Tommy would be the kind soul who loved our snowman building even though we lost every year. That was never his focus; he just enjoyed spending time with me. For as much as I think he's an idiot in most aspects, I could actually learn a thing or two from him.

"The loved ones who submitted the names always include a small donation that continues to fund our annual Santa Day activities," Aracely continues. "This year, we raised over two thousand dollars thanks to your generosity."

Another cheer.

"As in years past, the tree will light up, and I will read the list in its entirety while the Maple Park High School band plays for us." Aracely points to the side of the stage where I assume the band is sitting. A slow and soft melody fills the air right as the tree lights, and the crowd claps. Even in the morning sun, all the lights are illuminating. The tree always manages to take my breath away.

Aracely waits a moment before she starts to read, starting with her grandfather, "Larry Hernandez."

Tommy leans over to me and whispers, "I didn't get Grandma a light. I feel terrible. She always wanted a light."

"Roger Hannover. Myrna Marsh. Annette Scott…"

"We couldn't have known, Tommy. We'll get her one next year."

"No, let me finish. I called Aracely about it, and it turns out she had already had an anonymous donation and a light for her."

I make eye contact with Aracely right as she announces: "Butch Thomas. Elisabeth Thomas. Bryan Thomas." I suck in sharp breath, and my throat tightens. I don't have to guess who put Grandma's name in, tucked right between my grandfather and father.

As the rest of the names are read, I glance around the crowd, searching for something to ground me so I don't finally cry at the exact moment I don't want to. Everyone is listening intently. A few people have begun to sway with the music. I see Pete toward the front holding one of his kids on his side. A few of the older kids, too hyped up to sit on Santa's lap, are inching toward the Legion doors.

When one kid is finally brave enough to make the move, he opens the door, and I catch a glimpse of the inside. It looks exactly how it used to. Decorations, complimentary snack table, chairs and tables for socializing, kids' games for entertainment, and of course, mistletoe.

I find myself gravitating toward the door, pulling Tommy with me. Aracely finishes reading the list to a loud round of applause.

"C'mon, Tommy," I urge. "Let's get Niko and Otis on Santa's lap."

March, twenty years ago

"Aracely," I call as soon as I burst through the front door to her mom's house, barely remembering to shut the door behind me. "Cely," I repeat, dodging in and out of rooms in the small ranch style home.

"Eli?" I hear Jasmine, Aracely's mom, ask from the kitchen. I head in there and see she's making homemade tortillas. Instantly, I salivate. Taco nights in the Hernandez home are unmatched. Her mom knows I love the chorizo and queso fresco combination, but I can't handle the heat of her homemade salsa just yet, so she makes me a special plate every time I come over. Aracely definitely inherited her love of food and all things culinary from her mother. "You're a little early for tacos, *mija*."

"It already smells so good in here, but that's not why I came over. Is Aracely upstairs?"

She wipes her hands on her apron and motions to the back patio. "She probably has her headphones on and can't hear you."

"Thank you." I step forward and plant a kiss on Jasmine's cheek before exiting through the sliding glass door into the backyard.

Her mom was right, Aracely is sprawled out on the patio furniture and lightly singing a pop song to herself. I move quietly until I'm right behind her and grab her shoulders with a loud "Gotcha."

She jumps and swings a fist out of instinct. When she sees it's me who has barely dodged her knuckles, she dramatically grabs her chest and pulls down her headphones. "Eli," she chastises and pauses her music. "You can't sneak up on people. You're gonna get your ass kicked."

I scoop her into my arms and pull her into a standing position. "Sorry," I whisper before kissing her. I pull away and put our foreheads together. "I like to keep the element of surprise."

She swats at my chest and pulls back just enough to look into my eyes. "Well, I'm surprised. You're early for dinner. I haven't even started the rice, what's up?"

"I got something in the mail today. Something big." I bounce in place, hardly able to contain myself.

She bounces with me. "College? Which one?"

"University of Minnesota. They wanna offer academic and athletic scholarships. On top of everything else, I'm probably going to get financial aid grants and my dad's death benefit. I will have tuition and room and board for free for all four years."

She picks me up and spins me around. "Baby, that's great!" She kisses me on the lips, then the cheek, the neck, my ears, and back to my lips. "I'm so proud of you," she whispers against them.

"Thank you," I whisper back. She releases me so I finally have full weight back on my own feet. "Have you heard from them? Minnesota?"

"Yeah, I was accepted. Not with all the accolades you were, but accepted. Actually." She steps back from me. "I was offered a scholarship from Iowa State, the Traditions one." Silence hangs between us for a moment. I'm not understanding what she's saying, so she has to spell it out for me. "I don't think I can turn it down, E. It's way too good an opportunity. I can double major like I want to and come out on the other end with little to no debt."

My face falls, and the smile I thought might be permanent turns into one of realization and disappointment. "But I thought—"

"We'll be okay," she interrupts and steps forward. Her arms circle me, and she kisses the tip of my nose. "We'll figure it out. This isn't going to be a problem."

"I got an offer from ISU, too. I can look in—"

"No." She covers my mouth. "No more of that. You're not

turning anything down. We're not making any rash decisions today, okay?"

She releases my mouth. "Promise me," I say quietly. "Promise me we will talk about this and work it out. I only want you. I don't care about which school I go to. I can be a writer anywhere."

She stays silent.

"Cely."

"I promise, Eli. We will figure this out."

She hugs me in an attempt to prove her words, but I can't stop the dread slowly filling me. Somehow, this feels like a moment that will define us, and not in a good way.

Excerpt from The Stone River Series by Eli Thomas

Book One: The Curse

Joey barely catches herself fast enough to brace against the stairway banister. Her hands can't catch up with her mind, but they do manage to find purchase in Sidney's hair that's actually being worn down and loose for once. Joey pulls back for a millisecond to catch her breath and then surges forward again, kissing Sidney with everything she has. Her lips move, her tongue flicks and drags, her teeth nibble. Sidney releases the tiniest moan, and Joey's knees almost give out on her.

She can't believe this is happening. After all the fantasizing about kissing Sidney and having convinced herself that Sidney is straight, it was Sidney who made the first move. The urgent kiss activated a wild, unabashed need inside Joey and set forth a manic make-out session that guided them through Joey's empty house and toward the bedroom.

Sidney pulls back and sucks in a breath like she's about to say something. Joey's immediate fears come to the forefront of her mind. "Is this okay?" She releases Sidney and moves back. "I'm sorry. I shouldn't have—"

"Don't do that. I'm the one who kissed you first, remember?" Sidney steps forward and pulls Joey in by the waist.

"Sorry, I just—"

"I want you. I want this."

"You pulled away."

"To ask you if you wanted me to slow down." Sidney laughs.

"I was getting a little handsy and a lot turned on. I don't want to overstep because—"

"I don't want to slow down." Joey shakes her head and then realizes she interrupted an important part, "Oh shit, I'm sorry. Again. Goddamn it." She brings her fist to her forehead. "I'm a mess. It's been a while. I'm sorry."

Sidney softly shushes her before softly kissing her nose and lips. "Stop apologizing. You have nothing to apologize for. Please relax and know that this is something I want. I was saying I don't want to go too fast because I have feelings for you. I don't want to ruin it with a one-night stand."

Joey's shoulders relax. She takes a steadying breath. "I want this, and I like you, too. No matter how far this goes tonight, I'm going to still want something tomorrow."

Sidney tightens her grip around Joey's waist. "Good."

Joey holds eye contact, intoxicated by her. She wants her with every ounce of her being. She's drawn to Sidney in a way she's never been drawn to any of her other lovers or girlfriends. Sidney is someone special, someone who will have the ability to shatter her heart, mind, and body for better or worse. Anticipation fills Joey from her fingers to her toes as a thrill runs through her. She leans forward.

"Kiss me again," she demands. "Take me to the bedroom."

"Anything for you, baby," Sidney practically purrs back.

CHAPTER TEN: THE FIGHT BEFORE CHRISTMAS

There are easily five hundred photos of the boys on Santa's lap before Tommy, Angie, Tara, Aracely, and I finally give another kid a chance. We grab the free snack bags from the back table and feign that they're for the literal infants we brought with us. Aracely nudges me and makes a joke about stealing candy from a baby. Tommy swears he just wants the peanuts, but I catch him digging through one of the bags for a chocolate Santa.

The boys aren't big enough to play any of the games, and the holiday movie won't keep their attention, so Angie and Tara offer to bring them to Grandma's house after they go home, eat, nap, and do whatever else needs doing. Tommy stretches and attempts to hold back a yawn while agreeing. After the kids are gone, I can't resist suggesting we go to BJ's for the hors d'oeuvres and happy hour specials.

Neither Aracely nor Tommy object to the idea. Once we load up our plates and order drinks at BJ's, I spot Pete and his wife at a high-top table with plenty of empty seats. He happily waves us over. We're all two drinks deep with full bellies when I do a quick check of my watch, and I'm flabbergasted to see it's barely an hour into the afternoon. I'm definitely going to need a nap to sleep off this buzz before the fireworks tonight.

After two more drinks, we all part ways for an afternoon nap. I wake up just in time for the boys to come over and Aracely to return. I'm watching the babies look around while lying on the living room floor when I get a text from Pete. It's an invitation for Aracely and me to come to their Christmas party that evening.

"Bring some snacks and one white elephant gift per person" are the only instructions.

After some digging in the basement, we find old Christmas records and used gift bags. Aracely makes sure to point out that old records are far too fancy to be considered for white elephant, but neither Tommy nor I will keep them, so it'll do.

The party is a blast. So many drinks and so much laughing that I think I may actually pee my pants. We dance, sing, play games, and drink some more. I eat so much food my stomach is pushing uncomfortably on the top button of my jeans. There are a few people I haven't spoken to since high school in attendance. They're all far too eager to ask so many questions about my life and about my books. The same Taylor twin from Grandma's visitation is there and had 3D printed tiny stockings for everyone as a party favor. Sara the cheerleader ended up marrying Asher, who was a part of our friend group, so apparently, she's in it now, too. I'm most thrilled to see Katie Lewis. She was the friend I was the closest with in middle school and up until I started dating Aracely. She lives in Chicago and works as a nurse now. She comes home for Santa Day every year.

As I do my best to catch up with anyone and everyone I see, every bit of timidity I had over seeing people from my past dissipates and is replaced by an amplified desire to do this more often. It's a whirlwind of a night to top off the whirlwind day down memory lane. I nearly freeze my ass off watching fireworks without the peacoat at nine p.m., then lazily walk home with Aracely by my side, who is also slightly drunk and without a coat. Right as we stroll through the front door of Grandma's house, she makes mention of promising her mom we'd help with the Christmas baking and wrapping donation gifts tomorrow. Under the guise of alcohol, I happily agree to it.

As she and I fall into my old bed, one we've had sex in many times before, I can't help but laugh at the whole situation. She pauses kissing my neck to ask me what's funny, but I just shake my head and encourage her to continue. Tommy is so deeply asleep

I can hear him snoring through the floor when we got home. I'm not worried about noise levels, especially since the boys went home with their moms.

I pull Aracely's shirt over her head, and she quickly discards my sweater before going right back to the side of my jaw. She pulls my head farther into her and latches on to the back of my neck, biting down. She's the only one of my exes who has found that spot, and she's clearly never forgotten what it does to me. My hips buck, and a moan trickles from my lips that echoes into the darkness of my room.

Her grip on my arms tightens as she doubles down and sucks even harder. She's definitely going to leave a mark. Another moan from me, louder this time.

She releases my neck and smiles against my skin. "Still the same spot."

I hum in response and make quick work of her belt buckle, very desperate to have her naked. I remember all her spots, too, and I'm not going to waste another second without showing her exactly how well I do. Sitting in my lap, she grinds against me, and I bite the top of her breast. She throws her head back and tightens her grip in my hair. After I know I've sufficiently marked her, I release with a pop, only to hear her labored breathing.

"Still the same spot," I tease back.

She breathes out a quick laugh and pushes me back onto the bed. "Take off your pants."

It's not until she has me naked, back arched, hands in her hair, and moaning a string of expletives mixed with her name, that I realize I just had a perfect day. It's during my second orgasm that I start to think about how I wished for this for so long, and it's just as good as I fantasized about so many times over the years. We've both gained some confidence when it comes to sex, that much is clear, but we have both also managed to remember what makes the other person tick.

I thrust my hips against her hand and silently beg my body to let me release so I can have the third happy ending to my day. Aracely's body goes rigid for the fourth time since I started coaxing her with my mouth, tongue, fingers, and grinding legs. I pause and hold both sides of her face so she's looking right at me.

She freezes, the tension between us too heavy for words. Without breaking eye contact, she maneuvers her body down mine and works her mouth against me until I build back up, arch, and release with her name on my lips.

She falls asleep pressed against me and naked under the heavy comforter. Her breathing has evened out before I can even whisper good night. I carefully reach out to grab my phone from the nightstand and accidentally bump the picture I still have facedown. I check the time and see it's past midnight. Christmas Eve. Normally, I'd be quietly coming into town on this day. Now I'll be waking up here in bed next to my high school sweetheart. I put my phone back and gently tip the picture frame back up so it's facing out. Two kids about to fall madly in love. I bury my nose in Aracely's hair. Now we're two adults who still can't seem to let each other go.

I'm ready to fall asleep adequately tired, full, and satisfied... and yet there's still a sliver of dread hiding beneath the surface. Just the tiniest morsel of understanding that this can't last forever. This isn't my life anymore. As much as I love these people and this place, I managed to outgrow it with time and space. Sure, I ran away at first, but I truly did build something for myself outside of Maple Park. Now I just need to find the balance of my new life and making sure I stay connected to the past.

❖

When I wake up, I'm alone in the bed, and Aracely's spot is cold. Dread floods me. Maybe panic. Did I do something wrong? Why would she just leave?

I fly out of bed and barely have time to slide on an old pair of sweatpants and a hoodie before I'm bounding down the stairs to find Tommy. Maybe he saw or heard her or something. I can smell breakfast in the kitchen right before I reach the last step. I veer right and nearly slip on the rug near the door.

"Tommy," I pant, coming into the kitchen. "Did you see Ar—"

I stop. Aracely is standing at the stove in my baggy pajama shirt and an old pair of sweatpants she must have found in my dresser. She looks so cute in my clothes that I can barely form a thought, let alone words.

"Yeah?" Tommy answers, coming from behind me. "Did you say my name?" He turns to Aracely. "That smells amazing. What is it?"

"I'm making French toast." She smiles. "Merry Christmas Eve."

My mouth is already watering as I plop down at the table.

"You are a goddess." Tommy sits next to me, and we watch Aracely plate our warm breakfast.

She serves each of us and then brings glasses of chocolate milk and a huge bottle of syrup.

"Where did you get all of this?" I ask in awe. "Did you plan this?"

She nods. "I mean, I hadn't planned on spending the night." She winks at me, and I feel my face go hot. "But I knew that Elisabeth always did this for you two growing up, so I wanted to make sure you had it"—she clears her throat, tears filling her eyes—"one last time."

I catch a weakening in myself, but Tommy wastes no time digging in and loudly moaning. "This is so good. Thank you, Cel."

I take my own large bite. The warm cinnamon toast melts in my mouth, and the syrup is so sugary that I catch myself smacking my lips.

Aracely makes a plate for herself and joins us at the table. "So, fam, what's the plan for today?"

"Well," Tommy says around a huge bite. "Mom is coming to see the boys, and then tomorrow, they're going to see their other grandparents."

"Mom's coming?" I ask, nearly choking on a bite. I reach for my milk to wash it down. "Again?"

"Yes," he replies quickly. "Wait, did you just say you spent the night?" He frowns at Aracely, who nods back at him.

She smiles at me, and I'm actually glad I can see a bit of

bashfulness in her. It's nice to know I'm not the only one who still gets squirmy and stupid over what we have.

Tommy looks between us. "You shit." He shakes his head at me and smiles. "I always knew you'd circle back around."

I punch his arm. I'm not exactly sure what he meant by it, but it felt like an insult, so I went with my default.

"Elisabeth Thomas." The scornful voice freezes me in place. "Don't hit your brother."

I turn to find my mother once again standing near the kitchen entrance.

"Mom, hi." I greet in the most monotone voice I can muster. "You're here early." This is the most I've seen my mother in *years*. As far back as I can recall, she's never visited this many times in such a short time span.

"Yeah, actually, you're way earlier than you said you'd be. The boys won't be here for a few hours," Tommy says apprehensively.

I glance at the clock on the stove and realize I slept in after my fun-filled day of food, drinks, and sex. It's already past nine, and I can't remember the last time I slept this late.

"That's okay, sweetheart. I actually came to ask Eli about this." She holds up the contracts from Rae about the prequel money and the miniseries scripts. I can clearly see the bright green sticky note she attached to the top of them inquiring about when we're going to move to LA. I knew someone had been in my room.

"Did you go through my stuff?"

She scoffs. "Not intentionally. I was looking for some old photo albums in your weird attic closet thing so I could compare Tommy's baby pictures to the boys'." She tosses the contracts in front of me. "Do you have something to tell us?"

"No." I grab the papers and refold them.

"What does it say?" Tommy asks.

Aracely stays silent, always respecting my boundaries.

Mom nose laughs. "Your sister is moving to Los Angeles, and she's going to be a millionaire with the amount of money she's being offered for another book and a movie."

"It's a prequel." I correct her. "And a miniseries." I hold the letter tighter. The anger building. "And I'm already a millionaire," I jab.

"Wow, that's huge," Tommy says. "Congratulations."

I'm waiting for him to make a dig about the house being his now, but it never comes. I look at Aracely, who appears to be sad but only smiles at me. "I can't imagine anyone more deserving. You've worked really hard and had to give up a lot for this."

She means I had to give up *her*. Except I didn't have a choice.

My defensiveness is growing. I clench my jaw.

"You're running away again," Mom predictably interjects.

"Mom," Tommy scolds her.

"What?" she asks, oblivious to her own rudeness.

"It's my decision to make," I state flatly.

"Of course," she agrees, "and you'll make the one that benefits you and only you. I can't for the life of me figure out why your grandmother left you this house knowing you'd never actually stay here."

"I don't know either, Mom, but you can't make me feel guilty for the actions of a dead woman. I didn't do this."

"So give it back to Tommy and take the damn car you want so badly."

"It's not his!" I stand, and the chair I'm sitting in tips backward.

"Eli," Aracely whispers and reaches for my hand. "It's Christmas Eve, let's just—"

"No." I yank my hand away, sick of everyone telling me how to act or what to do. "I left this town for a reason." I stomp away from the table and to the coat closet. "So I'm not going to move back just because of a house or nephews I didn't even know about or because you're still in love with me." I wave a hand at Aracely. "I don't know why she left me the house, but it's mine. I'll do with it what I want, and I don't have to stay to see it through."

"Eli!" Tommy stands. "Don't—"

"Shut up, Tommy. You could have called. You could have told me she was fading, but, no, you just let me go on believing this Christmas would be normal." My voice cracks, but tears still elude me.

"Normal?" He practically shouts back at me as I slide on a coat and hat. "We haven't had a normal holiday since you left, E. Believe it or not, we missed you. We wanted you here."

"You have a really funny way of showing it. Never a phone call. Never a visit. Hell, I was lucky if I got a text from you on my birthday."

"That door swings both ways," he replies calmly and without a hint of arrogance. It pisses me off more.

I finish dressing and slam the closet door. I carefully take in the three large sets of eyes staring back at me. They're waiting for something. An apology, probably, but it isn't coming. I'm already so deep into this selfish shit fit, I may as well see it out until the end. It's not like I'm staying here anyway. "I don't belong here. I think we all agree. I'm leaving after tomorrow. Merry Christmas."

I look at Aracely, who has tears in her eyes, and regret my words. I feel a faltering in me, a moment where I hesitate and don't even believe my own voice. I pause and almost, *almost*, take it all back. Until I hear my mother's voice.

"Predictable."

I roll my eyes. "Mother of the year. As always." I turn and leave through the front door, not bothering to even close it.

❖

I'm aimlessly driving like I was just a few days ago when Aracely found me in the park.

And then kissed me senseless by the Christmas tree.

That won't be happening this time. Not after what I just said.

She told me she would love me until the end of her life no matter what because I'm her person.

I told her she's not worth moving home for.

She deserves better than me.

Tommy does, too. I'm not much of a sister. I'm even worse as a friend. I haven't even attempted to get back to Rae. And before this unusual month back home, I hadn't bothered to reach out to Pete. Not when he got married. Not when his kids were born. Nothing.

I know I have flaws, but the more I consider it, the more all these sound like someone I already know. Someone who abandons. Someone who uses anger as a weapon. Someone who blames others for their own problems. Someone who rolls their eyes. Someone who…is my mom.

I punch both feet on the brake so hard, the car fishtails, and the tires squeal on the pavement.

I take a few deep breaths that quickly turn into gasps for air. My knuckles turn white on the steering wheel. One of my gravest and deepest fears comes bubbling to the surface. I'm turning into my mother. No. I *am* my mother.

And not the version of her I want to be. Not the version who kissed my forehead before bed and ran her fingers through my hair when I felt sick. Not the version whose smile reached her eyes and was always laughing and fun. That woman died with my father. I lost two parents the day he was buried and was left with a new version of my mother who's angry, resentful, and wallows in self-pity. She's mean and judgmental. She drinks too much and wants everyone around her to feel that pain, too.

She's…

She's me.

My chest heaves. This path I've been going down, this path of anger and hate. This greed to always expand and to never let anybody get close for fear of losing them…it's exactly what she does.

I slow my breathing and loosen my grip on the wheel. Multiple pieces of the puzzle finally slip into place, and a rush of realization floods me. I flip my blinker to turn out of town toward the cemetery where my grandmother is buried. I figured it out. I know why she switched the will.

Christmas Eve, eleven years ago

Grandma is lazily pushing the cart through Wendell's, not looking
for anything in particular. She told Tommy and me that she just
wanted to get out of the house for a bit today before everything was
closed tomorrow, and she wanted us both with her. It has become a
bit of a tradition on Christmas Eve to go for walks or long drives,
or now, when her legs don't work as well, stroll through the aisles
of Wendell's for last-minute snacks before they close early for the
holiday.

Years ago, when we first moved in with Grandma, we discovered
that Santa Day makes her so happy and reminiscent of Grandpa and
Dad that the following day has become a grief hangover where she's
just a bit sadder than usual. She perks back up as we inch closer to
our Christmas Eve movie tradition. When we were younger, Tommy
and I would build a fort in the living room and pack it with snacks
and blankets and pillows to watch whatever movie we argued
over the least. Grandma climbed inside with us at first, but as she
aged, she resorted to watching from the couch. Ever since I left for
Minnesota, we've all curled up on the couch or in the recliners, but
I do think she misses the days of fort building.

Tommy is dragging his feet behind us down every aisle, barely
functioning and yet to take off his sunglasses. It's irritating me to the
point of breaking my sanity. I turn and snap at him. "Jesus Christ,
Tommy, are you really that hungover?"

He grunts. "Ask me again, and I'll vomit for you."

I roll my eyes. "You don't need to get wasted every Santa Day.

It's annoying." It has been an issue the last few years. Whatever girlfriend he has at the time is usually hanging around complaining of a headache, too.

"Sorry I have friends and a social life, unlike you. It's a town celebration. I'm an adult. I'm allowed to have fun."

"Yeah, looks like you're having a blast right now," I mumble.

Grandma pats the hand I have resting on the cart. "He's young. Let him have his fun before his hangovers last days instead of merely hours."

I glance behind me and see that he has stopped to observe the display of chips. I turn back to Grandma. "He should know better. Mom drinks like that."

Grandma sighs and turns down the candy aisle, her favorite. "You can't punish people for the mistakes of their parents. Just because your mom has an addiction doesn't mean Tommy will, too."

I know she's right, but I'm too irritated to care. I came home two days ago and fully planned on attending Santa Day to see some people I haven't seen since I left town. Every year, I get texts from a few old friends asking if I'm in town and if I want to get drinks at BJ's after the parade. I either don't respond or turn them down. I was always nervous about Aracely being there or being asked about her. But this year is different; this year I'm a published author. I have some money coming in. Some notoriety. I have a serious girlfriend that I am probably going to marry. I was ready for the messages, the invites, the excitement that I was home.

It never came.

Not even Tommy invited me to join him for anything. Tommy, who has been by my side since the day I entered this world, has written me off. I should be upset. Sad. Devastated, even. I avoided and said no one time too many, and people forgot about me. I am not worth the invite anymore.

Instead, I am pissed off.

Sure, I left because I wanted to run away from a broken heart. But look what I did. Dead father, addicted mother, broken relationship. I rose from the ashes like a goddamn phoenix, and nobody even appreciates it.

I grab some chocolate-covered raisins and practically spike them into the grocery cart.

"Do you want to talk about it?" Grandma's soft voice comes from beside me.

My eyes well with tears, but I refuse to look at her. "No." I tighten my jaw.

"You seemed pretty lonely last night. You didn't even come outside for the fireworks."

"Because I've already seen them. Santa Day is for kids. I'm not a child anymore." My tone is bitter. I deserve to be slapped on the mouth, but she would never do it.

"Honey—"

"I know. 'The only way out is through.'" I mock a sentiment she once shared with me.

Tommy slowly comes around the corner with a bag of chips in hand. He looks up, past us, and says, "Oh shit. Eli, don't look."

Which, of course, makes my head snap to the end of the aisle. There stands Aracely. She's shopping with someone.

Someone who is clearly her girlfriend.

Aracely has her arms wrapped around the girl from behind and is whispering something in her ear that must be comedy gold, judging by the dumbass giggle that escapes her.

I don't look away, but I respond to Tommy. "I don't care."

"We can go the other way—"

"I said I don't care," I say so loudly that Grandma jumps. I step forward and get in Tommy's face. "I don't give a shit about this town. About these people or the traditions, any of it."

He finally pulls his sunglasses off his head. "Jesus Christ, Eli. I was just trying—"

"Just stop." I glance back at Aracely, who is now gaping at us and the scene I'm making. It's the first time we've made eye contact in years, and my stomach bottoms out.

"I want to go home," Grandma says calmly. "Put the things back, we're leaving."

"God, Eli, now you've upset Grandma. Why does it always have to be about you? Huh? You get so mad when Mom does this shit, but you're just like her." He throws the bag of chips at my chest. I let it hit me and fall to the floor without an attempt to catch it.

Grandma is actually crying now as Tommy grabs her arm and guides her to the front of the store.

"Eli?" Aracely's voice is close.

I refuse to turn. I walk forward without acknowledging her.

"Eli, wait," she calls after me, but I speed up. The tears in my eyes are finally spilling over as I practically run to the exit. I don't turn around. I don't say anything to anyone on my way out, not even when Wendell himself wishes me a merry Christmas from behind a cash register.

I run outside, past Tommy and Grandma, and start down the street. "I'll walk home," I say through a choked sob.

"Eli, wait," Grandma pleads.

"No," I call back. "I'm leaving tonight."

CHAPTER ELEVEN: MISTLETOE

I've been sitting in the cold snow for hours now. Luckily, I had a bag chair in my trunk, so I'm not ass on the ground and soaked to my skin. My borrowed coat, gloves, hat, and boots have kept me tolerably warm while I sit here and spill my guts to a dead woman's grave. My toes have gone numb, and my fingers are starting to sting, but I've been far colder with way less clothing in the past. The adrenaline is what keeps me here and keeps me talking into the cold as puffs of my breath fill the air around me.

I'm telling her everything. Everything I've been keeping from her for years. Every detail of how I felt when I left town. How important Rae is in my life and how much I regret leaving everything here behind. I tell her that I loved her endlessly, even though I didn't show it enough. I tell her about my exes and how I almost married one of them, even though Grandma knew nothing about her. The more I unfold my life, the more I realize how much I kept hidden. So much time wasted. So much pain left unresolved.

I want to hate myself more, but realizing it out loud is doing the opposite. I'm finally allowing myself to heal. Grandma didn't leave me the house so I'd be trapped here; she left me the house so I could come home to be whole again and to give me a chance to make good choices. Ones I couldn't make in just a day or two. She forced me to stay and talk to people. Talk to my brother. Talk to my past. She left me the house so I'd actually pause for one damn minute and just *think* about it.

I'm out of breath and about to collapse from the cold when I finally admit, "I need to go home. I need to warm up." I stand and fold up the chair. I shake a few times to get the blood flowing back to my extremities. "I'm sorry I never said this out loud before." I pause and take a painful deep breath. "I loved you so much, Grandma. And I miss you so, so much." I look at the headstones of my grandfather and dad next to hers and think about a time when losing Dad was the most painful thing I could imagine. I healed, though, with time. I still miss him, sure, and I'm sad he's not around, but I can take a deep breath and think of him fondly without feeling like I'm also going to die from the pain of his absence.

Someday, it'll be the same with losing Grandma.

The only way out is through.

I turn and take a few steps before quickly turning back. "Oh, I forgot to tell you, Aracely made your kringla for Santa Day. It wasn't as good as yours, but it was close. It was really cute seeing her so excited to do it for you." My voice catches, and I feel my chest tighten. "She also got you a light for the memory tree. She—" Tears build and finally, finally fall. "She's such a good person. I'm so glad you had her here when I left. I promise that next year, I'll make your kringla and get the light for the tree. I'll do it every year that I'm able. I promise. I swear on everything, Grandma. I won't mess this up."

I turn again and see Aracely about fifty feet behind me, approaching with apprehension. I'm not sure if she heard anything from my confessions, but I also don't care. I'm so glad to see her that I could burst. I take a few steps forward and call out, "Hi."

"Hi," she responds and closes the gap between us. "I'm sorry if I'm interrupting." She stops right in front of me and wipes the few tears left from my eyes. "I was getting worried. You disappeared for so long, and you didn't have your phone."

"How'd you know where to look for me?" I pull her close and lean our foreheads together.

"Lucky guess," she whispers. "I looked quite a few places before here actually," she admits. "I'm not sure what brought me here. Just a gut feeling."

I pull back and look at her. "I'm so sorry."

She doesn't say anything at first, just searches my face. I'm not sure exactly what she's looking for, but she must see it in my eyes. Her features soften, and she smiles.

I pull her closer. "I have a lot of apologizing to do, and you're the top of my list." Even in the cold, with my body to the point of pain from the sting of it, I can feel her warmth radiating toward me. I love this woman with all I am. I always have. I always will. And I can't wait another second to tell her that. I cup her face, and she smiles at me like she knows what's coming. I find the arrogance of it even more endearing. "I don't know what's going to happen next. I truly don't have a plan figured out, I just know you're a part of it, Cely. It's always been you. It will always be you. I will love you until the end of this lifetime and into the next one and the next one and the next one. It's me and you in every dimension, every universe, and in every story. It's us."

She leans forward and rests her forehead to mine. "I love you, too. Always."

"I have a confession."

She pulls back and meets my eyes. "What?"

"I found the picture of us that you keep in your desk with the mistletoe and the letter you never sent me."

Her cheeks turn a deeper pink than from the cold alone. "You read it?"

"Yes."

She covers her face. "Oh my—"

I pull her hands from her face. "I was a little surprised you kept it in such an easily accessible location. Ashley was the one who told me about it."

"Oh, God." She buries her face against my shoulder. "That's so embarrassing."

I laugh and guide her face back so I can look at her.

"It was at my house, I swear. I had taken it to school because I was working on that letter during my free period. I had no idea a student knew—"

I kiss her rambling lips. "I wish you'd said all those things sooner. It was something I needed for years, but I realize now that I also needed to grow on my own. Thank you for making the hard choice that I couldn't back then. I know you did it out of love for me, even though it hurt you."

Her arms envelop me, and she squeezes so tight, I lose my breath. I can hear her voice break as she tries to speak. "Eli, I never wanted to hurt you. I never *wanted* to let you go. I know I chose money over you, but I swear that will never, ever happen again."

"I know." I tighten my grip on her. "We have time to talk through this later. For now…" I pull back and wipe under her eyes. "It's almost Christmas. We need to go help your mom with all the cooking and presents like we promised."

❖

I spend the rest of the day with Aracely and her mom. We bake cookies and prepare soup for tomorrow. We talk and laugh until my face hurts. I feel completely at ease and somehow manage, for the first time I can remember since being a child, to find the Christmas spirit within me. In the afternoon, I find time to shower, borrow some of Aracely's clothes, and wrap presents to be taken to the donation location for kids whose parents are struggling to provide.

When we get back to her house, it's past dinnertime. I sigh. "I should probably get home to Tommy for the rest of the night. He has the boys."

Jasmine drops the spoon she was using to taste test the soup for tonight's banquet at the church. "It's been so nice having you here all day, Eli," she says. "It felt like the old days when you two would help me out over school breaks with everything." She wraps me in a big hug.

I relax into her. It makes me miss Grandma even more, and oddly, makes me miss my own mother. I look at Aracely over her shoulder. She mouths the words, *I love you.*

Once I get bundled up to head back home, Aracely walks me to the door. "Will you come over after church?" I ask with just a hint of begging in my voice.

"Yes, of course. I'll come see everyone. Plus, I have a present for you."

I bounce excitedly. "Tell me what it is."

"No way. You have to wait until midnight."

"I will be asleep by then."

"I know," she whispers and leans forward for a soft kiss. "But it'll be Christmas."

I sigh. "Fine. But you have to wait for your gift, too."

She raises her eyebrows, obviously surprised that I wrapped something for her. It's Grandma's old recipe box filled with all her cards. Aracely is the only person who will ever truly appreciate it and put it to use. I'm so excited to give it to her that I almost, *almost* say it out loud.

"I will wait for Christmas morning. Are you coming to church?"

The look I give her must be hilarious because the laugh that bursts through her lips is immediate. "No, I will not be attending tomorrow's service," I say with the driest voice I can manage.

"Okay." She leans forward and kisses me gently. "I'll see you afterward. And tonight."

"Perfect." I nuzzle the side of her face and feel such a deep, overpowering love for her that I'm almost surprised I remember how. "See you soon."

She walks me a few steps to the door and grabs my shoulders to halt us both. She motions upward, and my eyes follow the path.

Mistletoe.

I look back at her and see the mischievous glint in her eyes. She waggles her eyebrows.

I shake my head and smile before leaning in and capturing her lips once more.

❖

When I get home, I can see Tommy sitting on the front porch swing and gently swaying back and forth. My throat tightens at the sight. We used to sit out here with Grandma on Christmas Eve and swing while staring at the sky. She had us looking for Santa and sipping hot cocoa with peppermint sticks. I get out of the car and slowly make my way up the walk and stairs. I silently motion at the spot next to him, asking for permission. He nods.

I take a seat and push us into a rhythm. "You see him yet?" I joke.

"Not yet. Might be too early."

"You'll have to do this with the boys in a few years."

He turns his eyes back to the sky. "Definitely." There's a comfortable silence before he turns to me. "I think you may have been right about Tara and Angie. They were awfully cozy on the couch in there while Mom and I were playing with the boys."

I laugh. "I honestly didn't expect to be right, but that's actually quite perfect for both of them."

He breathes out a long, relaxed breath. "Yeah, it is. I'm happy if they're happy. And you were right, it'll make things a lot easier on me if they're getting along and on the same schedule with drop-offs and pickups and all that business."

"Well, cheers to you and your gay baby mamas. I hope they never break up."

"Don't even joke about that. It would be a nightmare." He pauses for a moment. "Did you have a good day?"

"I did. I went and saw Grandma, and then I was with Aracely and her mom all day."

"That's great, E. She makes you happy."

"She does. She always has."

He nods and laughs to himself. "Did you ever think it was kind of odd that Grandma's poem she wrote for you said she wanted to be cremated, but her own funeral plans she made with Lara had her buried in a plot next to Dad and Grandpa?"

I snort and shake my head. "Always keeping us on our toes." We swing for a moment in silence before I finally muster enough courage. "I'm sorry about what I said, Tommy."

He waves me off. "We all have weak moments."

"This was a pretty bad one," I argue, thinking he shouldn't let me off the hook so easily.

He nods. "Can I ask you a favor?"

I turn to him and raise an eyebrow. "Sure."

"It's not anything to do with the house or the will or your future plans. I know we'll figure all of that out. But will you try harder with Mom? Be more patient with her?"

It's like he read my mind from earlier. I suck a long breath in through my nose and release it with a puff of warm air that materializes and evaporates in the cold air. I'm done making excuses for myself when it comes to her. My mom will find her own way in time, and even if she doesn't, she's my mom, so I will love her regardless. Especially since realizing that if I don't change something or choose to be better, I'm on a fast track to being cynical and miserable forever. Maybe all she needs to realize her own shortcomings is for me to be the one to give in. The strong one isn't the one who digs in their heels and holds their ground the longest. Strength comes from growth, and growth comes from realizing error. I only wish I had figured it out sooner.

"Yes, I will do better. I promise." My mom's heartbeat was the first thing I ever heard. We're connected whether or not either of us likes it, and I, for one, am done fighting.

He releases a shaky breath. I didn't realize how scared he must have been to ask that of me. "Thank you. I know it's not always easy with her—"

I practically spit out a laugh. "No, that it is not." I bump his shoulder. "But I will try harder on my end. Hopefully, it'll help."

He bumps me back. "So you're sticking around for a while?"

"Yeah." I sigh. "I think so. I need to finish updating this house. I don't know how long, but for now, I'm going to be here."

He smiles. "I'm glad. Merry Christmas."

"Merry Christmas, Tommy."

❖

I ask Mom to join me in the kitchen for a moment after Tommy and I go inside. She begrudgingly follows me after a quick argument about wanting to stay with the babies.

"Well?" she asks the moment we're alone.

My skin prickles and I feel my typical defensiveness rising. But I didn't ask her in here to fight. This is to start mending what's broken. "I'm sorry, Mom."

She freezes in place and whatever spat she thought we were about to have has effectively died on the tip of her tongue. "What?"

"I'm sorry. I'm sorry I'm not fair to you and that I don't give you a lot of grace. I'll try to do better."

"That's not what I expected you to say," she answers honestly, her eyes big.

"I know." I let the silence hang between us for a bit. I'm not sure what I'm waiting for. A returned apology from her, maybe? "Mom, why are you so hard on me?"

"What do you mean?" She shifts uncomfortably from one foot to the other.

My mother has darker hair than Tommy and me. She's also shorter than me, which may be intimidating at the moment, but her height has never stopped her big personality before. The wrinkles around her eyes can no longer be hidden behind the makeup she wears every day, and now that I'm taking the time to actually observe her, I can see her age more plainly than ever before. It reminds me of Grandma when we first moved in with her. I soften even further. "I mean that you are always very critical of me." I hesitate, debating if Christmas Eve is a good time to have this conversation. "Harder on me than you are on Tommy or anyone else."

She looks at her hands and swallows hard. She doesn't have to look up for me to know there are tears forming. "I don't mean to be. You just…"

"I what?" I prod, gently.

"You're always challenging me. The things I say. What I do. Even when I'm trying really hard to do something right, you have something to critique. I don't handle it the best, I suppose." She trails off.

"Sounds like we have the same problem." I attempt a smile when she looks up at me.

"I wasn't a very a good mother, I know that," she admits. "But those babies are giving me a second chance to be better."

I nod, finally understanding why I've seen her so much in the past couple weeks. Niko and Otis are her clean slate. "Well, let's make a deal, then. We will both try harder to be better with one another."

"What does that mean?" she asks, genuinely.

"Well, let's start with Christmas tomorrow and just trying to get along for Tommy and the boys? We can go from there."

She nods. "I'd like that." She hesitates a moment and then smiles at me. "You're a lot like her sometimes."

I frown. "Grandma?"

She nods. "Yeah. Don't get me wrong, you look like your father and you act like me, but there's definitely something distinctly Elisabeth about you."

I smile back. "Thank you for saying that." It's the best compliment I could have ever received from her.

Christmas Morning, thirty years ago

I finished my French toast and chocolate milk but stayed sitting at the kitchen table. I know it's Christmas morning, and I know I should be excited because I just opened presents, but I can't help feeling guilty about Mom. It's our first Christmas without her.

Tommy has retreated to his bedroom with his new CDs and speakers. I should be doing the same, but I just can't find the will to move.

Grandma takes the plate from in front of me. "You okay, dear?"

I don't look up.

She doesn't move. My lips curl downward, and the tears fill my eyes. I shake my head as they start to streak down my cheeks. "I miss my mom. The old her, the one she was when Dad was here."

Grandma pulls a chair closer to me and sits. She starts rubbing my back, so I put my head down on my arms. "She'll find her way back," she says. "It just might take a while, and she might not be exactly the same when she does." She pauses and then barely says, "The only way out is through."

"What does that mean?" I frown.

"It means that the only way to heal from a hard time is to get through it. It takes time. Your mind, body, and soul have to do a lot of healing. Even when you don't realize it, you're doing the work. Crying is progress, pain is progress, everything is progress. It just takes time."

"I hate this," I blubber. "I want things to go back."

"It also means that things can't go backward, honey." She

straightens her shoulders and perks up. "But we can help control how they move forward."

I sit back and wipe my eyes. "What do you mean?"

"Well, it's Christmas. How about we make some traditions for you, me, and Tommy? Some things we do every single year."

I consider it. "Yeah, I like that."

"I made French toast with cinnamon this morning because that's what I used to do for your dad when he was a little boy." I hear a catch in her voice, but she recovers so quickly, I don't have time to dwell on it. "Did you like that?"

I nod quickly. "Tommy did, too. He licked the syrup off his plate."

"Perfect." She smiles and continues. "Well, Santa Day will always be on December twenty-third. How about on Christmas Eve?"

"Build a fort!" Tommy comes into the kitchen. He must have been eavesdropping. "We used to do that with Dad. Build a fort of blankets and pillows and watch movies."

"Oh yeah," I agree. "Let's do that!"

"Can we do it today?" he asks Grandma. "Since we missed it last night."

"Of course." She claps her hands. "Let's get started right now. I can do dishes and clean the kitchen tomorrow. It's Christmas!" She stands and puts my plate back on the table. "Tommy, go grab all the blankets you can carry from the chest in my bedroom."

"Okay," he says as he turns and runs up the stairs.

"Eli, you pick the first movie."

"Yes." I turn and hold my hand up for a high five. Grandma doesn't even hesitate to oblige. I laugh. I love when she's goofy with us. "What do you want to do for tradition?" I ask as we walk to the living room and look for the TV remote.

"Well, I think we should watch for Santa on Christmas Eve."

"Definitely."

"And always eat lots of kringla."

Tommy comes bounding down the stairs with so many blankets,

he can't even see. "Watch movies and eat all day. That's the best Christmas," he calls out from behind the stack in his arms.

"Yeah. That's perfect." I grab half the blankets. "Can we move furniture around?"

"Of course," Grandma says like it's the most obvious thing.

Without a word, Tommy drops the rest of the blankets and runs to the kitchen. "I'm going to grab these chairs."

Grandma runs her fingers through my hair. "Are you feeling a little better now?"

I nod.

"You're always going to miss what's been taken from you, but just remember that you'll find love and support close to home, okay?"

"Thanks, Grandma."

She straightens her posture. "Home isn't always a place, either. Sometimes it's a person or the people who mean the most."

I meet her eyes. I know this moment is important, and her words hold meaning that I don't quite understand yet. "Okay," I reply. "I'll remember."

"Now," she motions to the pile Tommy had left behind, "let's find the biggest blanket."

Excerpt from The Stone River Series by Eli Thomas

Book Two: The Oracle

Abby practically tackles Joey in a hug when she finally sees her again. "I was so scared you were dead," she says into Joey's dirty, ripped, and bloody hooded sweatshirt.

Joey squeezes her with all her might, which isn't much at the moment. "As always, I appreciate your candor."

"Don't ever do that again," Abby mutters.

"For the love of everything, I hope I never have the opportunity to do it again." Joey laughs because at this point, there's nothing else to do.

Abby steps back and wipes her eyes and nose. "Where's Officer Cruz?"

Joey tosses her head in the direction of the broken-down squad car and the FBI circling around it. "She's over there about to hand some people their own asses."

Abby looks and snorts. "Good. They need it." She turns her focus back to Joey with a somber look. "Did you find out anything about Mason? Or the curse?"

Joey sighs. "A lot, and at the same time, not enough. The seer was right about quite a bit, but the curse is still here, and Mason is still lost."

"How do you know?"

Joey points in the distance at the River Hills. Abby gasps when she sees the black smoke billowing into the air. "Is Mason up there?" She takes a few steps away.

Joey catches her by her arm. "No, he's not. He's not here, Abby. Not in this realm."

Abby nods like she understands, but Joey can tell there are still gaps in all this for her. "Can we stay here? Please? I don't want to leave Stone River again. This is our home."

Joey pulls her in for another hug. "We're staying. This isn't over yet, and Sidney needs our help. Plus," she pulls back and looks at Abby, "nothing beats the feeling of being close to home."

Five months later, present day

Aracely kicks her tangled legs out from under the sheets, effectively revealing my naked chest.

"Hey," I protest. "I was warm under there."

"Look!" She flashes her phone in my face, completely ignoring my whines.

I squint at her screen, but I can't get my eyes to focus quite yet. "What am I looking at?" I finally ask. I can hear Potato groan from her bed on the floor. She's also not ready to be awake.

"Eli," she practically squeals as she sits up and thrusts the phone closer, as if that will help my eyes focus. "It's a job offer from the traveling food blog."

"No way. Baby, that's amazing." I wrap my arms around her waist and pull her back down on top of me. She kisses up my face.

"It's a risk." She sighs, and I can tell she's already terrified of what this means. She applied for the job over two months ago almost as a joke when she found the posting online to replace one of their United States travelers. The interview process was actually quite harrowing, considering how little money she was being offered. It was almost like she'd just be working for notoriety. She loves food, and with the advanced palate she has, it's a dream job for her. "It pays shit. Literal shit. It barely covers travel and food, and it's only guaranteed for one year of work. They're giving me the cities and places to go see and write about."

"We talked about this," I reassure her and kiss her face again. "I have money. Let me take care of you while you figure this out. I can write on the road. We can see this beautiful country together." I squeeze her tighter. "I'm so proud of you."

She lies back down and traces the side of my face with a single finger. "I'm in love with you."

"Falling forever." I squeeze her.

Aracely's finger traces down the side of my neck until her hand finds purchase on my chest. "I'm sorry it took me so long—"

I shush her. "We're done apologizing, remember?" It's a pact we made after the first few weeks of us deciding to give this another shot. It's hard not to constantly say those words knowing I hurt someone I love. Aracely felt the same, so we promised each other that all was forgiven, and we're looking forward now. The only time we look back is to reminisce.

"I'm going to accept it." Her hand flies to her mouth, and her eyes bulge. "I can't believe I said that."

"It's perfect timing. Summer just started, and you didn't sign a teaching contract for next year."

"Gosh, Pete was sad that day."

"Baby, look at me." She focuses on me. "Let's do this. Let's take the risk together. I've told you before, I can be a writer anywhere. I want to be with you, location doesn't matter." I stretch my arms high above my head and release a sound of relief. "Plus, I just sent my first round of edits back to my editor. I have about six weeks before I need to focus on that."

Aracely stares at me for a moment and kisses my cheek. "I'm so proud of you for finishing it. I knew your motivation would come back."

"You helped." I pat her hip. "This is going to be fun."

She squeals and kicks her legs again. "Can Potato come, too?"

"You know I can't go anywhere without my little spud."

She takes a few deep breaths, but she can't stop smiling. "Okay, I need to talk to my mom. We need to pack light since we'll be moving around a bunch. Oh man, we need a vehicle. What should we take, mine or yours?" She waves an anxious hand in front of her own face. "I'm getting ahead of myself. That doesn't matter yet. We need to pack first."

"What day do we need to be on the road?" I ask through a yawn. As anxious as she is, I'm extremely relaxed and happy about this.

"In less than a week." She sits straight up again. "Good thing my mom is dating that guy now. He will keep her company. And oh my gosh, the boys! We will video call them every day."

"I don't even see them every day right now."

She jumps out of bed and frantically starts looking for her clothes. "I need to go home and sort things out. You pack. I know it'll be easy for you since you never really unpacked the stuff from your apartment." She barely manages to award me another glance before she leaps into the bed, kisses me again, promises to love me until the end of time, and sprints out the door and down the stairs.

I rub the remaining sleep from my eyes and roll to look at Potato over the edge of the bed. "You ready to be a traveling pup?" She yawns and rolls over to request a belly rub. "I can't reach you from here, goof."

I slowly find my way out of bed and into some clothes before meandering down the stairs. Tommy is in the kitchen eating his cereal. I tip my head at him. "G'mornin'."

"Aracely ran out of here like she was on fire."

I pour a generous cup full of freshly brewed coffee. Somewhere along the line of finishing renovating the house and moving what I didn't sell from my apartment back to Maple Park, Tommy and I found ourselves a nice little routine and a way to coexist in this space. Even if it is temporary. "Yeah, she got the job. The traveling one."

He stops chewing and slowly looks up. "So what does that mean?"

"It means I'll be moving my stuff to the room in the basement finally. It'll be storage and a place to stay when we come to visit. All the rooms upstairs will be for you and boys."

"Wow." He takes another bite. "Finally ready, huh?"

"Yeah, sorry I stayed for so long this Christmas."

"Really outstayed your welcome," he jokes. "Not very Midwest of you."

❖

At the end of the week, after we said tearful good-byes to everyone, including my mom, it's just Tommy and me standing on the front lawn and staring at the house. It looks fantastic. New paint, new windows, the basement is fully finished, and the floors are all redone. Tommy and I worked our asses off this spring, and we definitely spent way too much money doing it.

But nothing is as superb as Dad's Starfire. Tommy completely restored it and added a new paint job to make it red and white, just like Dad wanted. As we stand on the lawn and admire the house we grew up in, Tommy turns to me. "Renovated house."

I glance behind me at Aracely loading the last bag into the Starfire with Potato waiting at her feet to be put in the back seat. "Restored car," I say back.

He holds up the keys. I take them and gently hand over the keys to the house. We went to Lara's office yesterday and made the switch official and legal. "Do you think this is what she planned from the beginning?"

"Yeah. She wanted us to talk. To fight. To have to actually compromise and work through something together, and—"

"She wanted you to find your way home again," he finishes for me.

I look at the house. "It was never about the house. It's you. Aracely. The boys and even Mom. You're my home."

"Wow," he breathes. "That was corny."

I playfully punch his chest. "You're corny, asshole."

"That's enough crying for today. Get in the car and call me later."

"I will." I give him a quick hug, then push him away.

I join Aracely in the car and turn the key to bring the beast to life. Potato is already curled up in the back seat on her bed with a toy and a bone.

I put the car in drive and slowly roll down the street toward the edge of Maple Park. We'll be back in six weeks as we make our way back from the West Coast and head east. Aracely has an entire itinerary set for her. I have my laptop and a writing schedule to meet for the prequel I agreed to. The prequel didn't seem so daunting once my passion reignited for the series. I even started outlining it as I was finishing the third book. I signed the contract the same day Rae arranged with the publisher to sell the concept for my series to Netflix under the agreement that different writers can adapt the scripts. I will be credited for the original story but won't be obligated to write anything or oversee any of the creative ideas. I was perfectly happy to relinquish that side of it. I'm actually excited to see what someone else does with it.

As I inch toward the city limits, Aracely takes my hand and squeezes lightly. "I'm so glad we're doing this together this time."

I squeeze back. "Me too."

I turn my attention back to the road just in time to see the now leaving Maple Park sign with a request to come back soon. This time, I know I actually will.

Three years later, three days before Christmas

Aracely insists that there is no way we can honeymoon in Greece for two weeks because we can't possibly leave our precious Potato for that long.

"Seriously, Cely, I'm about to just buy Potato a plane ticket. This would be the trip of a lifetime."

"When we went to London last summer, my heart nearly expired from having to leave her for only a week," she says over her shoulder as she pulls open the door to Pump It.

We both walk in and stomp the snow from our shoes. "She would be staying with Tommy," I argue. "Hey, Harper," I toss to my right. "And she'll be just as spoiled with him as she is with us. Plus, the boys will be there more than a few times to play with her."

"Hey, guys," Harper says without looking up from her phone. "Heard you two got married. Congrats. 'Bout time."

"Thanks, Harper," Aracely says loudly from the back wall where she's examining which drink to buy. "Eli wants me to abandon our sweet baby to gallivant around Greece, but it's fine."

"Jesus Christ." I rub my eyes. "Tommy's new girlfriend loves dogs. She'll be there, too," I call out without moving from my place in front of the register. I turn to Harper. "How have you been?"

She sets down her phone and looks up. "All good. Not much has changed since I saw you two last Santa Day."

"Has my mom been around?"

"Oh yeah." She yawns and stretches. "Met her boyfriend. He seems nice. Is she moving back here?"

"Yeah, I think she might." My heart swells slightly. My mom and I still have our differences and continue to argue often, but she's really taken her role as a grandma seriously. She's genuinely trying to be great for Niko and Otis, and I am actually proud of the progress she's made.

Aracely returns to my side and puts down five drinks on the counter. I turn to her with raised eyebrows and motion to the display of beverages before me.

She shrugs. "I couldn't decide."

I kiss the side of her head. "Anything for you." I turn my attention back to Harper. "We'll be taking all five of these."

Harper smirks at Aracely and starts to ring up our purchase. "I read that you were hired by an online magazine to keep traveling and reviewing."

Aracely straightens her shoulders with pride. "I was indeed. I'll be housed in the Midwest now, though. We might even be able to put down some roots somewhere." She bumps my shoulder. "Get Potato a yard to run around in."

"I'll consider it if you consider Greece."

She huffs. "You know I'm going to say yes. We're going to Greece, I just can't think about it right now. I already miss her, and she's sitting in the car."

"Did you bring kringla?" Harper asks as we gather our stuff and head for the door.

"Of course I did." Aracely beams. "I get closer to perfecting it every year."

Harper fist pumps. "Awesome. See you guys tomorrow at the parade."

I wave back at her and let the door close behind me. When I get back in the car, I blow on my hands for warmth. "Okay, where to? Your mom's house or Tommy's?"

"Neither." Aracely turns to me. She quickly glances at Potato, who is soundly sleeping in the back seat. "Let's go to the park and walk the trails to the gazebo and Christmas tree."

I lean toward her. "You wanna make out there?"

"Always." She closes the distance to lightly kiss me. "We have a lot to do the next three days with seeing the boys, my mom, going to the cemetery, and meeting up with Pete and his wife tomorrow night. I want to get a moment with just us. Just for a bit."

I gently bump our noses. "Maybe we could also go looking for some mistletoe with a purple ribbon?" I suggest.

"Yes, please." She leans in to kiss me again, but we're interrupted by a grunt from the back seat. Potato sits up and pokes her head between us. I scratch under her chin. "That all might have to wait. We need to get this one to the house first." I sit back in the driver's seat and fasten my seat belt. "Ready?"

"Ready."

Excerpt from The Stone River Series by Eli Thomas

Book Three: The Remedy

Sidney steps forward to help secure Joey in her bulletproof vest. She yanks a little too hard on one of the straps. "Whoa, tiger. I need to be able to breathe." Joey laughs.

"Sorry, I'm just really glad you decided to wear it this time." She leans in and kisses Joey's cheek.

"Yeah, I definitely don't want to catch another bullet." Joey presses her forehead to Sidney's. "Or get possessed. Or break my collarbone."

Sidney snorts. "Better yet, maybe you should sit this one out."

"Never." Joey swells with a pride she never knew existed. "I feel like this might be my calling. Part of my destiny or something." She looks at Sidney, who doesn't respond. "Never mind, it's stupid."

Sidney cups her face, "Don't do something silly or reckless just because you think this is your fate. I don't want to do this life without you. Whether it stays wild and unpredictable or it gets quiet and boring, I just need you to be in it."

Joey links an arm around Sidney's waist and uses the other to push her loose hair away from her face. "After this, it's you and me, okay? I have some big plans for us."

"Oh really?"

"Yeah, really. I love you, Sidney Cruz." Joey kisses her but pulls back almost immediately, thinking better of it. "Actually, I'm in love with you."

"What's the difference?" Sidney asks as she places a soft kiss on Joey's jawline.

"In love means I'm falling. And I just keep falling and falling deeper and deeper in love. It never stops. You're it for me. You're my great love." Joey pulls Sidney into her for a tight hug.

"Well, in that case, I'm in love with you, too, Joey Campbell."

"Falling and falling?"

"Falling and falling forever, baby."

Joey leans back and kisses Sidney. "Great, now that that's cleared up, let's get in there."

"Are you two done grab-assing over there?" Rex calls from across the warehouse. He's armed to the teeth, rearing and ready to go.

"Anxious to get back to that old teaching job, Rex?" Sidney calls back.

He takes a few steps toward them and laughs. "I would rather drag my head across the carpet until the skin burns off my face than go back into education."

"Jesus," Sidney says. "Gross."

Joey looks past Rex and sees that everybody in their ragtag group is ready to go, including Abby. She's not sure if they're waiting for a speech or some direction, or are just ready to get to what they all hope is the final battle. She turns back to Sidney. "You ready?"

"Ready."

About the Author

Allisa Bahney grew up in a small town in northern Iowa. She works in education and has a master of science degree in teaching with minors in creative writing and film studies. She lives with her wife, kids, and dog near Des Moines.

Books Available From Bold Strokes Books

Close to Home by Allisa Bahney. Eli Thomas has to decide if avoiding her hometown forever is worth losing the people who used to mean the most to her, especially Aracely Hernandez, the girl who got away. (978-1-63679-661-1)

Innis Harbor by Patricia Evans. When Amir Farzaneh meets and falls in love with Loch, a dark secret lurking in her past reappears, threatening the happiness she'd just started to believe could be hers. (978-1-63679-781-6)

The Blessed by Anne Shade. Layla and Suri are brought together by fate to defeat the darkness threatening to tear their world apart. What they don't expect to discover is a love that might set them free. (978-1-63679-715-1)

The Guardians by Sheri Lewis Wohl. Dogs, devotion, and determination are all that stand between darkness and light. (978-1-63679-681-9)

The Mogul Meets Her Match by Julia Underwood. When CEO Claire Beauchamp goes undercover as a customer of Abby Pita's café to help seal a deal that will solidify her career, she doesn't expect to be so drawn to her. When the truth is revealed, will she break Abby's heart? (978-1-63679-784-7)

Trial Run by Carsen Taite. When Reggie Knoll and Brooke Dawson wind up serving on a jury together, their one task—reaching a unanimous verdict—is derailed by the fiery clash of their personalities, the intensity of their attraction, and a secret that could threaten Brooke's life. (978-1-63555-865-4)

Waterlogged by Nance Sparks. When conservation warden Jordan Pearce discovers a body floating in the flowage, the serenity of the Northwoods is rocked. (978-1-63679-699-4)

Accidentally in Love by Kimberly Cooper Griffin. Nic and Lee have good reasons for keeping their distance. So why does their growing attraction seem more like a love-hate relationship? (978-1-63679-759-5)

Frosted by the Girl Next Door by Aurora Rey and Jaime Clevenger. When heartbroken Casey Stevens opens a sex shop next door to uptight cupcake baker Tara McCoy, things get a little frosty. (978-1-63679-723-6)

Ghost of the Heart by Catherine Friend. Being possessed by a ghost was not on Gwen's bucket list, but she must admit that ghosts might be real, and one is obviously trying to send her a message. (978-1-63555-112-9)

Hot Honey Love by Nan Campbell. When chef Stef Lombardozzi puts her cooking career into the hands of filmmaker Mallory Radowski—the pickiest eater alive—she doesn't anticipate how hard she'll fall for her. (978-1-63679-743-4)

London by Patricia Evans. Jaq's and Bronwyn's lives become entwined as dangerous secrets emerge and Bronwyn's seemingly perfect life starts to unravel. (978-1-63679-778-6)

This Christmas by Georgia Beers. When Sam's grandmother rigs the Christmas parade to make Sam and Keegan queen and queen, sparks fly, but they can't forget the Big Embarrassing Thing that makes romance a total nope. (978-1-63679-729-8)

Unwrapped by D. Jackson Leigh. Asia du Muir is not going to let some party-girl actress ruin her best chance to get noticed by a Broadway critic. Everyone knows you should never mix business and pleasure. (978-1-63679-667-3)

Language Lessons by Sage Donnell. Grace and Lenka never expected to fall in love. Is home really where the heart is if it means giving up your dreams? (978-1-63679-725-0)

New Horizons by Shia Woods. When Quinn Collins meets Alex Anders, Horizon Theater's enigmatic managing director, a passionate connection ignites, but amidst the complex backdrop of theater politics, their budding romance faces a formidable challenge. (978-1-63679-683-3)

Scrambled: A Tuesday Night Book Club Mystery by Jaime Maddox. Avery Hutchins makes a discovery about her father's death that will force her to face an impossible choice between doing what is right and finally finding a way to regain a part of herself she had lost. (978-1-63679-703-8)